M000036422

of **GUILT** and

INNOCENCE

JOHN SCANLAN

of GUILT and INNOCENCE

FIRST SUNBURY PRESS EDITION
Printed in the United States of America
December 2012

Trade Paperback ISBN: 978-1-62006-178-7
Mobipocket format (Kindle) ISBN: 978-1- 62006-179-4
ePub format (Nook) ISBN: 978-1-62006-180-0

Published by:
Sunbury Press
Mechanicsburg, PA
www.sunburypress.com

Mechanicsburg, Pennsylvania   USA

Author's Note

It should be noted that while I used the names of actual police departments I did take some liberties with the layouts of those departments (size, number of investigators, etc.). The policy and procedures I depicted came from my own personal experience or knowledge of procedures I am to follow, rather than the procedures in place by those specific departments depicted. Despite these small changes I tried to remain true to the emotions of the investigators and first responders and the actions they would take.

For my lovely wife, Jessica, whose support and faith has never wavered; and my beautiful daughters Alexandra and Taylor, who provided me with the intimate, first-hand knowledge of a father's love for his daughter. Without that I never would have been able to do this novel justice. This is dedicated to the three of you with all of my love.

Acknowledgments

As the idea of writing a novel finally struck me as "not impossible" and I began down this path, I decided I would keep this plan and subsequent workings a secret to all. But as my undertaking progressed, my secret endeavor gradually grew less covert. And as more people learned of what I was doing or had done more people helped in ways I can't even begin to express profound gratitude for. But I will try.

First and foremost, I am beyond fortunate to have had guidance from accomplished author Bill Kauffman. He was always willing to promptly and kindly answer all of my menial questions and respond to every single one of my emails, all of which began "Hey Bill, quick question for you" (which of course was followed by neither a quick nor singular question). His advice and encouragement provided me the desire to continue. Thanks Bill, and go Muckdogs!

Gratitude must also be expressed to my publisher Lawrence Knorr, who saw it fit to take a chance on a police officer whose only previously published works were seen in the booking blotter of the local newspaper.

A very special thank you should be extended to the Palm Beach Police Department's Director of Public Safety Kirk Blouin, Detective Larry Menniti, and all the men and women of the Palm Beach Police Department for their support.

I wish I could mention everyone here who has encouraged or helped me along the way, but unfortunately I cannot. To anyone I missed, forgive me and please accept my heartfelt gratitude.

—John Scanlan

CHAPTER 1

She should have come inside by now. Lisa's brow furrowed as the house's silence seemed to indicate she had not. Thinking perhaps she had missed Ashley's entrance, Lisa called out to her daughter from her position in the living room but got no response. Frustration built as she pulled herself up off the couch and walked to the back sliding glass door she had unlocked for Ashley. She was not really concerned, just angry that her daughter had not obeyed her wishes.

"If she's ruined those new shoes already I am going to be pissed," she said aloud to herself. That was her main concern when she had granted the anxious five year old permission to retrieve the mail from the mailbox as they had pulled into the garage. She feared Ashley would play with her toys in the yard rather than pick them up, another condition of her mail retrieval request being granted, and would get the very new, very white patent leather shoes dirty. They weren't expensive really, but they were the only purchase of the three hour mall excursion from which they had just returned and she wanted them to last slightly longer than most of her daughter's footwear.

Lisa opened the door and stepped out onto the large wooden deck, scanning the backyard and surrounding horizon. There was no strawberry blonde girl in patent leather shoes anywhere, and the toys she had been tasked to recover still sat in the same places. Lisa again called out to Ashley, and once again she got no response. She walked down the deck steps into the backyard and checked the side of the house, calling to Ashley the entire time. The side of the house soon became the front of the house, and still, there was no sign of her daughter. Lisa's barefooted steps now matched the frantic pace being set by the beating of her heart. She had soon made an entire revolution around the house with nothing to show for her efforts.

The anger she initially felt at what she believed was wrongdoing by her daughter was quickly replaced with panic and confusion. She ran back to the front of the

1

house, frantically calling for Ashley, pleading with every scream for her daughter to show herself and end this nightmare before it truly started. She continued down the street until she reached the main gate of the housing community in which they lived; still her efforts were unsuccessful.

Fear consumed Lisa and she ran back to the house to retrieve her cell phone from the kitchen counter. She hurried back outside as she dialed her husband's cell phone number, which went straight to his voicemail. She tried him again and again, the call going to his voicemail every time.

Lisa was becoming desperate; she checked the garage, under the deck, inside the house, everywhere she could think of, but still no sign of Ashley. Twenty minutes had now passed since Ashley had jumped out of the car to fetch the mail and her toys and Lisa knew something was wrong. It was unlike Ashley to wander off. Never once had she left the yard on her own, or even asked if she could other than to ride her bicycle in front of their house, and Lisa had seen the princess bicycle with streamered handles still propped up on its kickstand in the garage.

Something was most definitely wrong, she was certain of it, but she was frozen, not knowing what to do about it. She hesitated to call the police. In the back of her mind there was that thought that she was overreacting, that she wanted to speak with her husband, Tom, first to see if he had a better idea of where she could be or how to go about looking for her. She didn't want to be "that mom"; the one who freaks out over any minor misunderstanding. She tried to call Tom's cell phone again, but again it went straight to voicemail.

Lisa went back inside, trying to remain calm. She looked up the phone numbers of the parents of Ashley's friends within the gated community on the chance that her daughter had ventured out on her own for the first time to meet them. As she called them, three in all, she tried to sound as if nothing was wrong and it wasn't a big deal. But one by one each parent told Lisa that Ashley was not with their child, and she fell into despair. She couldn't focus; too many thoughts fluttered through her mind.

2

She strained to think of anywhere else Ashley could be, but she drew a blank. Tears began streaming down her cheeks. Twenty five minutes had now passed since she last saw her little girl. Something had to be wrong, something horrible had happened—but it couldn't have; not to her, not to her family. Not in her part of Boca Raton, the only part that mattered. She'd lived in Boca Raton all her life and could never imagine such a thing happening there. She knew full well that bad things did occasionally happen in Boca Raton, but not in the part of town in which she was born and raised. And definitely not in the picturesque gated community in which they now lived. Kidnappings only happened on TV, to people you don't know who live in trailer parks or communities of extreme wealth in California or the Midwest. It couldn't happen here, the place she felt was safe.

She struggled with these thoughts, becoming more and more anxious. Finally, unable to wait for her husband to answer his phone any longer, she dialed 9-1-1 and pleaded with the voice on the other end of the line for some help.

Two squad cars pulled up to Lisa, who stood in the driveway, after what seemed like a lifetime of waiting. Still sobbing, she struggled to compose herself enough to tell the officers what had happened. One requested that Lisa go back inside with him so the two of them could check for Ashley there. The other got a description of Ashley and what she was wearing—a white short-sleeved shirt, blue jeans, and, of course, a pair of white patent leather shoes— and began driving around the neighborhood looking for her. An exhaustive check under every bed and in every closet of the house failed to turn up any new information, and Lisa plummeted further into hopelessness. She was finally able to get through to Tom, who had turned off his phone while he golfed, just as he always did. His Saturdays were generally spent at the local country club, of which he was a member.   Lisa struggled to find the words to describe what was happening and simply blurted out, "Get home now, something happened to Ashley."

Tom's heart was racing; he tried to remain calm as he drove, but that proved to be impossible. When he finally arrived the sight of four police cars greeted him. He jumped out of his Lexus as quickly as he could and ran inside to put together the rest of the partial story he had been told. He saw Lisa sitting on the couch, crying, her shoulder being gently rubbed by the female police officer sitting beside her. A male officer was also in the living room, standing beside the couch, writing something on a clipboard. Lisa sprang up when she saw Tom and embraced him, sobbing uncontrollably. "What happened?" he asked in a soft tone, worry projecting from his eyes. Lisa couldn't stop crying long enough to explain. She tried several times but couldn't calm herself in order to get the words out. Tom felt tears well up in his eyes as he hugged her. Was his daughter dead? Had there been an accident? The officer with the clipboard slowly walked over to him and looked into his eyes, trying to give a comforting half smile.

"Mr. Wooten, my name is Sergeant Mike Stokes; this is the information we have so far." He said in a practiced soft, gentle tone. "At approximately one-twenty this afternoon your wife and daughter returned from the mall. Your daughter wanted to get the mail, and so your wife allowed her to. While your daughter was getting the mail, your wife went inside your house, got changed and waited for her to come in, but apparently she never did. Your wife went outside to check on her and discovered her missing—that's when she called us. Right now we have two officers in patrol cars checking the area. We have two officers on foot going door to door. Her description has been broadcast all over the county and officers have been told to be on the lookout for her. Detectives will be here soon to start their investigation just in case this turns out to be something more than she just wandered off. A crime scene unit will be here as well. So far your daughter has been missing for forty-five minutes." Though he tried to maintain the calming tone, his words came out sounding very matter of fact and robotic.

Sergeant Stokes had been a patrol supervisor for roughly seven years, but had never supervised the preliminary investigation into a child abduction, which made it hard for him to accept that it could, in fact, be a legitimate abduction. He really believed in his heart that the girl would be located and it would be discovered that she had simply wandered off; he just hoped she would be found alive and well. "We are going to do everything we can to find her," he added.

The back of Tom's neck felt like it was engulfed in flames. His mouth was suddenly overrun with saliva and his eyes lacked focus. He questioned silently how this could have happened. It had to be a mistake. Missing? It just couldn't be possible. He stood almost paralyzed as he held his still sobbing wife. Just then a tall, heavyset white man and short, muscular black man, both dressed in suits opened the front door and walked into the foyer area, standing there sheepishly. The heavyset one motioned for Sergeant Stokes to approach them, which he did.

"What do we got here, Sarge?" he asked. The men were the Boca Raton Police Department detectives that Sergeant Stokes had promised would arrive and he repeated to them the information he had just told Tom Wooten.

When the briefing was finished the shorter detective asked the all-important question, "Do you think this is a legit kidnapping?" Both detectives were well aware that in the typically crime free, wealthy areas of Boca Raton crimes of this magnitude tended to get sensationalized by the people who reported them.

Sergeant Stokes looked at him and shrugged, "I don't know Dan. I can tell you the girl is missing, but did she get taken by someone or did she wander off? I don't know. Either way there is a concern for her safety." He didn't want to say what was in his gut because if he gave the indication it was not a legit kidnapping and in any way hindered the initial investigation in doing so, he would surely face the repercussions. The three men approached Tom and Lisa, who were now standing in the kitchen, each drinking a glass of water. The tall, heavyset detective lumbered toward Tom with his right hand extended.

"I'm Detective Jim Brekenridge, and this is my partner, Detective Dan Jones. We understand this is a very difficult time for you folks right now, but we really need to ask you a few questions so we can find your daughter as quickly as possible." His tone was not as sympathetic as Sergeant Stokes' had been and a sense of urgency came through in his words. Jim's approach to police work, and social interactions in general for that matter, was no nonsense; his bedside manor was less than comforting most of the time. He would not hide his anger when he felt people were wasting his time; however, no case he was given and instructed to solve was ever too small to receive one hundred percent of his attention.

"Uhh, sure, yeah, ask whatever you need." The first words out of Tom's mouth since learning of his daughter's disappearance sounded odd as they hit his ears. They didn't sound like they were spoken in his voice, and they seemed reluctant as he moved his lips.

"If it's OK, sir, I would like to interview you in the kitchen area here, and my partner can interview your wife outside, maybe? It will be easier and quicker, and that way she can show him the places she looked and take him through everything she did prior to our arrival." In actuality, the detectives simply wanted Tom and Lisa separated. If there were any pertinent details that may cause trouble between the spouses, they were most likely to come out with the parties out of earshot of each other.

Tom and Lisa agreed and Lisa exited the residence with Detective Jones following behind. Tom and Jim sat on barstools at the kitchen counter next to one another. Tom explained that he had been golfing with his brother, Mark, from ten that morning until he received the call from Lisa around two p.m. He explained that his Ashley had never wandered off before and, though she did have friends within their community, it seemed highly unlikely she would pay them a visit without telling her mother first.

"All right, I'm going to ask you this question and I really want you to think about it. Please don't take offense to it or anything, but also really consider it. Is there anyone, for any reason, you can think of who may have taken your daughter?" Jim studied Tom's expression as he asked this question. He watched closely for any tells or hesitation.

"No, no one." Tom responded after a brief moment to ponder it, nothing discernible in his body language.

6

"OK, well here is what I would like to do. First, I would like to get you to sign this form." Jim produced a piece of paper from the pages of his notebook and put it on the counter in front of Tom. "It gives us permission to search your home and have the Crime Scene Unit process it as a possible crime scene. I don't think we need to tap your phone lines or anything like that just yet, although we can't rule out the possibility of some type of ransom." Jim tried to think of every possible angle to a case from the second he was tasked to resolve it. He was known for going overboard at times: tapping the phone lines, or even requesting the department do it without any indication of a kidnapping for ransom scenario. He was teased for it by the other detectives often. They would ask why the National Guard wasn't called or other similar remarks. None of it bothered Jim though. He always felt it was better to act too soon than too late, and when his methods worked it made him look like a genius. Which, of course, he constantly reminded everyone of.

"Ransom? We don't have that kind of money. Who would possibly try to get ransom from us?" Tom was shocked. Kidnapping Ashley for ransom money seemed absurd to him.

"Well, you own your own business, you have this beautiful home . . . people might get ideas about your finances." Tom's was a small shop in a local strip mall in which he repaired computers, as well as selling individual computer parts or entire computers he had refurbished. The beautiful home, as well as the country club membership, was paid for mainly by the success of that business.

Jim noticed Tom looking over the form he had given him to sign. He knew Tom was having reservations about signing it and allowing the intrusion into his privacy. "Listen, our goal here is to find your daughter, that's all. We aren't insinuating that you or your wife have done anything wrong. We just don't know what happened, and until we exhaust every avenue it will be more and more difficult for us to do our jobs. We are going to search the interior and exterior anyway, this just allows us to begin right away without waiting for a search warrant. Unfortunately we don't have the luxury of time."

Tom signed the paper and slid it back in front of the detective.

Dan stood on the sidewalk with Lisa, who was still barefoot and with her arms crossed, having finally composed herself as best she could. She explained to Detective Jones everything that happened from the time she left her home to go to the mall to the time she discovered Ashley missing. He was trying to transcribe word for word everything Lisa was telling him in a small notebook. Dan Jones did not have the eight years of experience as a detective or the seventeen years of general police work experience his partner had. He had been a police officer for seven years, and a detective for only two. Dan was the mirror opposite of his partner in almost every way. Physically they looked nothing alike, with Jim being tall, heavyset, and white and Dan being short, thin, and black. Their personalities were even more diverse. Where Jim could be loud, crude, and quite often lacked social graces, Dan was a quiet man, very polite and soft spoken. These were the differences that made them such an efficient team.

"Did anything or anyone stand out to you at the mall? Maybe you noticed someone following you or had a strange encounter with someone?"

Lisa retraced her entire mall outing in her head. She realized how focused she was on shopping and how little focus she had on her daughter or anything else. She had always felt secure in her neighborhood and her home, as well as places she had been hundreds of times, such as the mall. But now that feeling of security had been stripped away. Tears trickled down her cheeks again as she felt waves of guilt wash over her.

"No, nothing" she replied, trying to catch her breath enough to answer amidst her tears.

"I noticed you have a security gate that everyone has to come through, did anyone or anything stand out to you as you entered the gate? Someone loitering in the area, or cars behind you that seemed out of place?"

"Not really, I wasn't paying attention when I got to the gate and I didn't push the clicker right away. Cars started lining up behind us; there were probably four, but nothing that would stand out."

Jim peeked his head out of the front door and motioned for Dan and Lisa to come back inside. Lisa sat down at the bar next to Tom as the two detectives conferred in private for a moment in the hallway. "All right, folks," said Jim in a booming voice as he and Dan re-entered the kitchen. "We are very sorry to be meeting under these circumstances, but for now that's all the questions we have for you. We will have more follow-up questions as the investigation develops, so we will be in touch." Jim paused for a moment to gather his things off the kitchen counter, then continued as if reading from a card or out of a textbook. "What's going to happen now is crime scene should be here shortly and they are going to process your house, inside and out, for any clues to your daughter's whereabouts. An officer will stand by with them while they are here. We are going to speak with the officers who are doing a neighborhood canvass right now and find out what information they have. After getting any pertinent information from them we will initiate an Amber Alert."

Lisa cried aloud upon hearing this. Just the words "Amber Alert" made it seem so real. It made her feel even more detached from her missing daughter and fearful she would never see her again. Issuing an Amber Alert was the modern day equivalent to the faces on the back of milk cartons she used to see when she was younger. Now the image she was envisioning on the back of a fictitious carton of milk was her own daughter's.

"Don't give up hope just because we are going to these lengths already," Jim said, sensing Lisa was becoming more hopeless with every detail of their planned investigation that he laid out. "There still is a good chance she could have wandered off and may simply turn up. But it is best for us to treat it as something more than that right now, just to be on the safe side, so we don't miss out on a possibly important piece of evidence by waiting. We are going to go run down some other avenues, but we will be in touch and we will keep you informed every step of the way. If there is anything you think of later on that might be important, please call us immediately. Nothing is too small. Also, before we go, if we could just get a recent picture of your daughter it would be very helpful."

Through a puddle of tears caught in her eyes Lisa looked at Tom, terrified. Tom knew what she wanted without her having to say it, and slowly walked into Ashley's bedroom. He tried to block everything out; just get the picture and be back out of the room as quickly as possible. What was once a happy place inside the house was now a virtual snake pit, full of memories that would serve to hurt if dwelled upon. Tom reached up and grabbed a picture frame off of a shelf. The picture, taken two weeks prior, was of Ashley holding the Wooten family dog in her arms and had been put in a frame and placed in Ashley's room just days ago. The look Ashley displayed was of pure happiness, a beautiful smile consuming her face. Though he tried not to, his eyes flashed across the picture, then slowly across her bedroom. He felt a pain like he had never felt before. Not the sharp, stabbing pain and shortness of breath he had felt when he learned his daughter was missing. This was a dulling pain that slowly became greater and greater.

He walked back out of Ashley's room, shutting her door behind him. He handed the picture to the detective without saying a word, then quickly walked into the master bedroom. The dull pain had finally consumed him. He sat on the edge of the bed with his back to the door and began to cry. Harder and harder he cried, still trying to be as quiet as he could. He knew he was going to have to be the strong one for Lisa. He knew he would have to remain positive and hopeful for Ashley. He just didn't know how he was going to accomplish those things, or if he even could.

The detectives and the Crime Scene Unit seemed to trade off with one another. Sergeant Stokes sat with Lisa and Tom, who had now re-emerged from the bedroom more composed. He ran his fingers through the sides and the top of his short brown hair, which he always kept well manicured— however, due to the excessive fingering it was now anything but. He stared blankly at the counter in front of him as he bit his lower lip nervously. He thought back to the last time he had seen his daughter. It seemed like an eternity ago, though it was just this morning. He had sat at the dining room table, which had a clear view through the glass doors into the backyard where she had been. He watched as Ashley ran and played and laughed. Her strawberry blonde hair was tangled and uncombed as it fell over her tiny shoulders. The sun shone down on her porcelain skin as she ran. He didn't know why, but at the time he could focus on nothing else but watching her. He remembered the hug and kiss she had given him before he left for his round of golf. He could still smell her shampoo and feel her soft skin. He still heard her voice telling him "Good luck" and that she loved him.

Now his heart was breaking and his stomach churned. Then he remembered something else. He remembered that as he sat at the dining room table, the few occasions when he was able to take his eyes off his daughter, he glanced at the day's edition of the *Palm Beach Post*. He remembered commenting to Lisa about an article that took up the bulk of the front page. It was about the serial killer known as the South Florida Strangler who had been terrorizing southern Florida for years. The article described the common belief that the killer had moved on in one way or another due to his body count remaining the same over the past six months. He had jokingly remarked about it to Lisa, feigning fright of the faceless killer. For some reason he thought back and felt a twinge of embarrassment over it now. Embarrassment for not truly seeing that the world could be evil. That evil things actually do happen in real life, not just in black print. He was certain that the so-called South Florida Strangler had nothing to do with his daughter's disappearance, ninety nine percent so, but someone else had still performed this unconscionably evil act—that much he was one hundred percent certain of. His fear was now real.

As Jim and Dan left the Wooten's neighborhood they felt the pressure that came with an investigation like this. They knew that it was very rare to find a missing child alive after forty eight hours had passed. For now, they still had time on their side.

They spoke with the officers doing the door-to-door canvass of the street and the officers driving the area looking for any signs of Ashley, but no one could offer any useful information. They were able to speak with the community property manager on their way out. He provided no positive information, only that there were no security cameras anywhere on the grounds and no one had called him about any suspicious activity today.

Two hours had now passed and Tom and Lisa still sat in their kitchen in disbelief. The hysteria that gripped them both in different ways had subsided a bit, but the worry and longing still had a hold on them. As crime scene technicians continued processing each room of the house, Lisa's tears gave way to anger and rage.

"Why are they looking inside the house? I told them she never came inside, someone took her from outside. Why are they wasting time in here?" Lisa's voice was a combination of desperation, anger, and annoyance as she glared at Sergeant Stokes and waited for an answer.

"We need to cover all our bases. We have officers all over right now looking for your daughter. Having crime scene look for clues inside your house isn't taking anyone away from looking for her. We just want to be thorough, that's all." Sergeant Stokes gave Lisa the same sheepish smile he had been giving since his arrival in the house. It was what he did when he was nervous. His response seemed to defuse Lisa's anger for the time being as she just nodded she understood and began sobbing again.

While Lisa, Tom, and Sergeant Stokes sat on the three barstools that lined the kitchen counter, sometimes making small talk, sometimes saying nothing at all, a knock on the front door came that made all three spring to their feet. Lisa tore off toward it, screaming "Ashley, baby, are you there?" Tom and the Sergeant followed close behind. Lisa opened the door and much to her dismay did not find her daughter standing there. Instead, a deputy holding the leash of a blood hound that sat at his feet stood before her. "I'm losing it!" She screamed and ran into the master bedroom crying hysterically.

The deputy looked heartbroken as he remained in the doorway. "I'm sorry," he said to Tom. "I know I'm not the one you were hoping to see. But Ranger and I are going to do our best to find your little girl. If you could just get me an article of her clothing, something she may have worn recently, we can get started." Tom turned and walked to Ashley's room's closed door. He stood in front of it for a few seconds with his eyes closed. He knew what torture it would be to go back in there again, but he knew he had to. He slowly crept in and grabbed the first thing that he saw. Quickly, he darted out of the room and shut the door behind him. He handed the K-9 officer a small pink blanket.

"She, uhhh . . ." His breathing quickened, "she uhh . . . slept with it . . . every night." Tom's voice became high pitched at the end as his hand rose to his eyes as he finished the statement.

"Great, thank you, I will get this back to you shortly." The officer placed the blanket in front of the dog's nose and gave some commands and words of encouragement to his four-legged partner.

The dog turned away from the front door and began a steady trot toward the mailbox. It then made a sharp left turn and began heading down the street toward an intersection. At the intersection, the dog and his handler turned left again and made their way to the front gate of the property. After getting the gate open the dog went to the end of the community's entrance way and made a right turn, heading south on State Road 441. After trotting a short distance southbound along the roadway, he lost the scent.

Jim and Dan were in the police department's substation within the Boca Towne Center Mall when Jim received the report of the police dog's findings. "She left the complex and headed south on 441," he whispered to Dan. "Looks like this one's legit."

"Great," Dan said aloud as he watched the security supervisor fumble with the controls to the closed circuit television in front of him.

The camera system at the mall encompassed both the interior and exterior and allowed for security footage to be pinpointed by time of day on each camera. Footage of set intervals of time could then be burned to a DVD. The detectives requested footage from every camera between the hours of ten a.m. and two p.m. All in all there were forty cameras between the common areas and parking areas, and there were even more they had yet to get information on from the individual stores Lisa and Ashley had entered.

After providing the detectives with the DVDs, the security supervisor also gave them the name of an individual who had caused problems at the mall in the past. He could not say for certain if the man was at the mall that day, but he had been there the previous weekend and had been reported to security by two women who felt he was following them. The individual had been ejected from the mall when he refused to obey any commands given by the crime prevention officers, and the actual police officers assigned to patrol the mall that day were called to assist in his removal.

The detectives made stops in each store Lisa had told Dan she and Ashley had gone in, and were able to obtain security DVDs from two of them. No one they spoke to at the mall gave any indication that they had observed Lisa and Ashley being followed, nor did they advise that they knew of any problems occurring at the mall that day.

Lisa returned from the bedroom and resumed her position with Tom and Sergeant Stokes at the kitchen counter. As the Crime Scene Unit finished their work and began packing up to leave, Sergeant Stokes stood up to accompany them out. "All right, I'm going to get going. If anything comes up at all, please call us. I gave you my card before, and it has the main phone number to the department. You also have the detectives' cards. Do not hesitate to call. If you notice or remember anything at all that might be important or if someone tries to contact you in reference to your daughter, no matter what they say, call immediately."

Tom acknowledged that they would and shook the Sergeant's hand and walked to the front door. As the door opened, a fair amount of people standing on the sidewalk across the street perked up. Several boom mics and cameras maneuvered for better angles.

"Damn it. And don't hesitate to call if these idiots start harassing you either," Sergeant Stokes said gruffly to Tom. The sergeant had placed one of his patrol officers in the front of the house while the crime scene techs worked. Because the early indications were that Ashley may have been abducted from the area of the mailbox in front of the house, that area needed to be left undisturbed until it could be processed, and so the officer had put up yellow crime scene tape that spanned the perimeter of the Wooten's property and all the way across the patch of road directly in front of their house. The media that had begun funneling in as the hours passed were told sternly to stay back from the tape and stay off of everyone's property, which left them relegated to the small strip of sidewalk.

Sergeant Stokes walked slowly down the front sidewalk as Tom quickly closed the front door behind him. Sergeant Stokes told the officer to remove the yellow tape and reopen the road after he and the crime scene units left the area, but to make crystal clear to the media outlets that stayed that they were not to be on anyone's private property or they would be arrested. The officer agreed and the sergeant lumbered forward across the street and to the edge of the taped off perimeter.

"OK, folks," he shouted, looking over the crowd. "We don't have a statement to make right now, but one will be forthcoming. I just want to remind you this family has been through a lot today and to give them the privacy they deserve in this trying time. Thank you."

With that, Sergeant Stokes turned his back to the media personnel and began walking to his car, ignoring the questions shouted at him. Soon the yellow tape was taken down and the media made their descent on the house.

As Tom walked back in the kitchen where Lisa still sat on a barstool, the cold truth suddenly hit him. They were alone. All alone. No police officers asking questions, no radios chirping. No technicians dusting for prints or looking for clues. More importantly, no child's laughter or constant questions. The eerie silence made the house seem lifeless and empty.

Fear gripped him again, but not the same gut-wrenching fear that had originally engulfed him when they realized their only child was missing. This was a fear of not knowing what to do, or what they should do. It bordered on guilt, not knowing what the "protocol" was in this situation to try to get their child back. Who would they ask? Who should they compare themselves to? They certainly knew of no one who had been in this position. Were they to become the people they had seen on news programs throughout the years? The people who made impassioned pleas on *Good Morning America*? Was that how these things were supposed to go?

"We need to look for her ourselves," Lisa said staring straight ahead, finally breaking the silence. "She's our baby, we need to be out there looking, not leaving it to the police."

"We need to call our families . . . they should hear it from us first."

"I don't care how they hear it, if I'm not out there looking, if I don't get out there to look today, I don't think I'll ever live with myself. I don't know how we sat here for so long without going out there and looking. What is wrong with us?" Her voice cracked again as her guilt again began to show.

"All right, let's go."

CHAPTER 2

Earlier that morning, a little farther south, in the town of Davie, the inhabitant of a small, muddled studio apartment struggled to rise from his pullout couch bed. A portly man, Louis Bradford stood only five feet six inches tall, but weighed two hundred and thirty pounds. He lived alone in that studio apartment, which was located above his mother's garage, while she solely occupied the property's main house: a modest, two-story home.

Louis staggered through the tiny apartment as he tried to shake off his slumber and prepare for the day ahead. He had lived in the apartment or the main house nearly all of his thirty seven years. The only exception came in his early twenties, when he spent two years away from his sanctuary in a Florida state prison in the town of Raiford.

In the main house his mother had been up for hours and was laboring to tidy up. At the age of sixty-seven Anne Bradford was worn down by life, both mentally and physically. She had very few personal indulgences or pleasures anymore. In fact, what made her most happy was still being able to take care of her only child. She had never resented Louis's refusal to work after his arrest, or that he had never shown an interest in moving out or starting his own family. She always turned a blind eye to his quirks, even as disturbing as they seemed. He stopped letting her come into his apartment years ago, saying he would clean it himself, though she knew he never did and at times the odors that would emanate from it were unbearable. She picked up on other things through the years she thought were odd but quickly suppressed those thoughts and move on. She never wanted to push him away.

His arrest and subsequent incarceration took a significant toll on her and continued still to have a profound impact on her life. People treated her differently because of it. Some blamed her openly for his behavior, while others who had been friends before his arrest avoided her all together after it.

Feeling winded already, Anne broke off the morning cleaning early and plopped herself down in a kitchen chair to rest. She suffered from a variety of medical conditions, but what had been bothering her most recently was her right hip. She had a replacement put in over ten years ago, but it was apparently beginning to falter and the pain was becoming unbearable. She had taken a leave of absence from her job as an in-home nurse for a hospice care company and had been seeing her physician regularly, discussing the prospects of yet another hip replacement surgery. Despite the gradually intensifying pain, she still took the bus wherever she wanted to go most of the time, which required a three block walk to the bus stop. Between the two of them they had only one car, an old blue 1995 Buick Le Sabre. However, if Louis needed the car at any point in the day, Anne would yield it to him; even though he never really had anywhere important he needed to be or go to.

The entrance to Louis's apartment was similar to that of an attic or crawlspace and Louis climbed down the wooden ladder that led from his apartment into the garage. He pulled open the old wooden garage door, jumped in the Le Sabre, and quickly backed the old blue jalopy out of the driveway. He made his way to Boca Raton, where he had decided to spend the afternoon at the Boca Towne Center Mall. He liked to spend most of his time people watching and had been to every mall in the area to partake in this hobby countless times. Boca Raton, Boynton Beach, the various malls in the Ft. Lauderdale and Miami areas; he knew the layouts of them all.

Despite his general poor hygiene and relatively unattractive appearance, Louis always dressed well when he left the apartment. Today he was dressed in a nice pair of blue slacks and a button down white short sleeved shirt. His thinning black hair was slicked back and he was clean shaven. He bore a loose resemblance to Alfred Hitchcock, with bulldog-like cheeks and a long, thin nose. He had developed skills as a chameleon over time. He could look very presentable, very kind and unassuming when he desired to give that impression. However, he had the capability of changing in a second and radiating evil— something he had done often over the past thirteen years.

Louis walked down the different corridors, looking more at the other mall patrons rather than the various stores. After completing one full revolution, he sat down on one of the benches and continued to watch. This routine had been perfected many times over. He was always discrete; he never leered or stared but just spanned his gaze and sat contently.

The mall was busy that day, too busy for his liking, so he walked to the exit he had parked closest to. Instead of leaving, he found a bench that faced the entranceway and continued his people watching from there. Finally, after a half hour of intently gazing at the herds of people entering the mall, two females caught his eye. An attractive woman with blonde hair hurried inside with a small, strawberry blonde girl at her side. Louis noticed how the blonde woman, although she was aware of where her little girl was, walked at a hurried pace and appeared to have her mind on things other than the child with her. Louis casually watched them as they passed and he began to follow at a distance.

The mother and child appeared to be oblivious that they were being stalked and they began to shop. The wheels in Louis's head were turning; he attempted to devise a plan unique to this situation, as he always had a general one in place. This was the reason for his trip on that particular day, the reason for all his trips, and so he always had a standard plan of action in his head, his modus operandi.

Louis observed the pair entering a shoe store. He positioned himself just outside the store's entrance and pretended to read and respond to a message on his cell phone. When the woman and her daughter exited the store, he noticed the small girl had on a new pair of shoes that were consuming her attention. He also realized her mother had not discovered this as quickly as he had. As the woman passed by him without the small girl by her side, Louis slid himself into the girl's path while she looked down at her shoes. The girl's head struck his large stomach and she fell to the ground. Louis quickly whipped his head around to observe the girl's mother and her reaction or if she had even noticed. When he observed the woman turn and begin walking toward her daughter, he quickly looked back at the girl who was staring back at him with fear and surprise. "I am so sorry," the woman said as she helped her daughter up off the floor.

"Oh it's no problem at all. I shouldn't have been standing looking at my cell phone on a busy day like today." He leaned down so he was eye level with the girl and asked in the kindest tone he could muster, "Are you OK, sweetheart?"

"Yes, sir, I'm sorry."

"It's OK, I'm sorry, too." He smiled at her and stood back up. A sense of satisfaction and excitement washed over him. "Well, have a nice afternoon," he said as he walked to sit down on a bench that had just become available. He was close; he could feel it building inside him. He watched the two as they walked away, hand in hand. He noticed how the woman began swiveling her head from store to store again, as if she had already forgotten the incident had occurred, or did not think much of it happening at all. Then he saw the little girl turn back and look at him. At first he saw a look of puzzlement, then, just before she turned her head away, he saw a look of calm, of trust. He had his mark.

With his target now determined, Louis continued to stalk his prey. For hours he would watch at a distance, calculating and recalculating his plan on how he would separate the woman from her daughter, or how he could strike if they became separated for any reason. But he soon realized a crowded mall was not the place to take action, and so he continued to just watch. He had become very patient over the years. He had been observing them for over two hours and felt strongly that their shopping day was almost over. He felt confident if he left right now they would soon follow, however, he hoped he would have enough time to get in his car and prepare for their departure without losing them.

He quickly exited the mall and did just that. From his parking space he had a clear view of the exit from which he knew his mark would come. Now, he would just wait. Fifteen minutes passed as he stared at the doors, hoping he had not been too slow. Finally, in a flash, a blonde woman holding the hand of a little girl darted out and very sharply walked to a blue Ford Expedition. Both were quickly inside the SUV and rapidly pulling out of their parking space, heading toward the parking lot exit. Louis backed out of his spot and put his car into drive.

CHAPTER 3

In yet another part of the Sunshine State that same morning, just a little farther south in the upscale city of Coral Gables, Carlos Hernandez was just settling down on a stool at his kitchen counter after his morning jog. As he sipped from a bottle of fruit punch sports drink, he spread out the day's edition of the *Miami Herald* on the granite countertop before him. The kitchen that surrounded him was lavish and gourmet. Not an expense was spared, despite the fact that neither he nor his wife cooked or entertained often enough to justify the opulence. It went well, however, with the rest of the gorgeous home nestled in the highly sought after Las Islas gated community. He began reading the *Herald* as he drank to replenish the electrolytes shed during his workout. After skimming its pages, he folded it up and set it back on the counter, replacing it with the *Palm Beach Post*. As he began reading the front page headlines, his wife, Julia, slowly emerged down the stairs.

"Did I wake you? I am sorry, I tried to be quiet."

"No, no, I woke up on my own," she said as she passed by him to the refrigerator.

"It says here that the South Florida Strangler is no more, left town, never to return," Carlos said with a large smile, exaggerating the real story. Being born in Cuba, he generally spoke with a slight Hispanic accent, but at times like this he brought it out on his own to make things sound more fantastic and emphatic.

"Good, that man is a sicko, killing helpless old ladies." Julia responded, not a trace of her Hispanic heritage to be found in her voice.

"How do you know it's a man? I have seen you very upset and can imagine you doing such things." Carlos looked back down at the paper as he spoke, he no longer had a smile, but it was clear he was joking. Words seemed to glide off his tongue whenever he spoke. People enjoyed listening to him talk, with his smooth Spanish accent and passionate way of describing a situation.

"I won't be home later. I have to check on a patient at the hospital and look at a few files. It may be a late night," he said, continuing to skim the newspaper.

Julia didn't respond to Carlos's advisement of his evenings plans. She had grown used to him not being around a lot.

As the morning progressed, Carlos retreated to his home office, somewhere he spent a lot of time over the years. It was a small room he liked to go in to think. He kept the lighting dim and had no television or distractions in it. The majority of the time he was in the office he would have the door shut so he had total privacy. It was a room all his own. It was his sanctuary.

He sat at a large dark oak desk and stared at an open medical file. Although his eyes did not focus on the words on the pages, nor did his mind process what the file said, he was thinking about this particular patient whose file lay before him, but in the abstract. He was picturing his encounter with her just the day before. An elderly woman, she had been coming to the office to see Dr. Morris for years, although Carlos had never seen her before he spoke with her yesterday.

She was having problems with her hip, which had been surgically replaced twelve years ago. He had consulted with her about it briefly, then gave her a ride home, which he found to be located in a very rough part of town. She seemed very matter of fact, very honest, however, her eyes told him a different story. He saw a look of guilt and a look of sadness in her eyes. After getting to know her a little bit he knew he shouldn't take this kind of interest in one of his own patients, but he couldn't help it; she was consuming him, what was in her eyes was consuming him, and he felt sorry for her. He knew what had to be done, he had done it many times before, but he wanted to be certain to make this one perfect.

And so he began to read, to study her file. He sat in his office for hours, reading it cover to cover, thinking, bulletproofing what he would do and how he would do it. As he thought and studied, slowly, a picture started forming in his head, a game plan. Piece by piece it came together, it developed like an orchestra slowly building, slowly adding more instruments, until finally, the crescendo. He seemed pleased with what he had formulated; he felt it would work. It would be perfect for her and her situation.

Carlos opened a locked desk drawer, the bottom one on his left hand side. He lifted a box of cigars up and placed it on the top of the desk. He then reached back down into the drawer and slowly opened the lid to another cigar box. He pulled an empty orange pill bottle out and closed his grip around it, staring blankly forward. After a few seconds his grip loosened and he read the name on the pill bottle, Elsa McMillian. He closed his eyes for an instant, as if to initiate the memory that came with reading the name. He smiled to himself, then slowly placed it back in the cigar box, alongside six other empty orange pill bottles. He shut the lid, put the box of cigars from the top of his desk back on top of the cigar box containing the empty pill bottles, and locked the drawer.

Carlos had a bit more studying to do to ensure the plan he had just developed would work. Perhaps there was still a minor detail or two that would require a tweak here or there. He opened a laptop computer that sat on the corner of his desk and pulled up the Broward County bus schedule. He found a starting location bus stop, an end location bus stop, a departure time after sunset, and a return time that he felt would work. If his plan was to be like that finely tuned orchestra producing a masterpiece he would have to do some reconnaissance work. After all, there was no margin for error; everything had to work perfectly. What Carlos was planning so methodically was not a hip surgery—he was planning to pick up where he had left off six months ago.

His first occurred by accident really; it was not his intention to have things end up that way and to get started down this path. It was back before he took his current position with a private practice medical office. He was working at Ft. Lauderdale Hospital as a general surgeon then and was asked by one of the oncologists there to speak with a woman who was having fears about having a benign growth removed. She was a woman in her early sixties who was having a hard time accepting that the growth being benign was a good thing. She had just heard the word surgery and became upset. She had requested to speak with a surgeon, and thus Carlos was brought in to ease her worries. Carlos used his smooth talking skills to set the woman at ease. He explained how a minor procedure like that was no big deal, he told a few jokes, smiled at her, and the woman felt comforted. She had already finished her appointment at that point, and so she walked out of the office with Carlos, who was also on his way home for the day. As the two walked and made small talk, she got her cell phone out of her purse and began to call for a taxi to pick her up. After some pleading, Carlos convinced her to let him drive her home. The two got into his car and drove to her residence, a modest apartment complex not far from the hospital. She lived alone, she explained, and though she did not drive, she tried to keep some of her independence, which was why she lived in a regular apartment complex and not a senior citizen community.

She thanked Carlos for the ride and offered him a cup of tea before he left, which he accepted. She sat next to Carlos at her kitchen table in the small apartment and asked him to describe the surgery in detail. He began to explain the intricacies of the surgery to her, looking in to her eyes as he spoke. He could see her vulnerability. A rush suddenly came over him and he looked away as he continued. His mouth was on auto-pilot, describing a procedure he had done many times before, but his mind was racing. He felt her helplessness and as he described the procedure he couldn't help but feel God-like. He felt like this poor woman needed him to keep her alive, that she was totally at his mercy, and that gave him a sudden rush of adrenaline and notions of power. The feeling of invincibility ran over him and he began feeling a strong sense of sexual arousal. It had never happened to him before, with a patient like that, but he did not have time to really acknowledge it. He was too overwhelmed by this sudden rush. It was not an attraction to the woman he was speaking to, but a feeling of power and control that had sparked his arousal.

Without thinking, he quickly placed his left hand on the woman's right thigh and squeezed, still looking away but no longer talking. He sharply looked at her as his hand continued to pulse.

The woman recoiled in surprise, quickly sliding away from him in her chair. "What are you doing?" She asked, surprised and scared. He sat there looking at her; his breathing and pulse had quickened, his veins still pulsing with adrenaline. His mind tried to process what had just happened, and he started to feel an anger wash over him. This was an old woman. He was a young, handsome doctor, and she was rejecting his advance? An advance he never would have made had he not been caught up in this sudden rush of power.

He could control his anger no longer and he lunged out of his chair, attempting to grab her. She managed to slip away and run to her bedroom with Carlos in pursuit carrying a large knife he had grabbed from a knife block that sat on the kitchen counter. Unable to shut the door in time, she dove across her bed and reached for the phone, but she never got there. As her fingers touched the top of the black handset that sat face down in its charger, the cold blade of her own kitchen knife slid into her back. She gasped as she lay there, still face down. Blood poured out of her wound and saturated her white blouse, then engulfed the floral bedspread on which she lay.

Carlos stood there in an almost trancelike state, the knife still protruding from the woman's back. Finally her gasps for air stopped and she lay still. It was as if, at that time, Carlos was finally awoken and he began to panic. He questioned what he had just done and tried to remember it all. He didn't understand the emotions he had felt or the reason he had so violently taken this woman's life, a woman whose name he did not even remember. But that wasn't important now. Now all he was concerned about was covering up this grisly act, and he began to think of how he could do just that.

He realized he had touched nothing in the bedroom as his forearm, which was covered by his white long sleeved shirt, had blocked the door from shutting. He made the decision that he had to take the knife with him when he left, and so he hovered over the woman's lifeless body and pulled it out, careful not to touch anything other than the handle. He then went back to the kitchen. He knew he could not deny being in the apartment; somehow, somewhere there would be a trace of him he would leave behind.

He decided to make it look as if he had finished his cup of tea and left, so he took both cups off the small table and put them in the sink, dumping out any of the excess tea. He then used a dish towel that hung from a small hook over the sink and began wiping the knife block he had taken his weapon of choice from in an attempt to remove any of his fingerprints he may have left there. Then, using the kitchen towel to cover his hands as best he could, he went through the woman's purse that sat on the table. He removed her wallet and placed it in his back pocket. He used the towel to wrap the knife, then he was faced with the biggest decision yet, how to get from the apartment to his car without being seen.

Luckily for him he only had a few small drops of blood on his shirt. Having only stabbed his victim once, and not very forcefully, reduced the amount of blood spatter he had to deal with. However, he would be carrying a rather large kitchen knife wrapped in a dish towel, and even just the sight of him walking to his car could be damning enough. But he didn't have a lot of options, and so he just went for it. He quietly shut the front door behind him and walked as quickly as he could down the hall, back down the stairs, and to his vehicle. It seemed as if he had managed to avoid detection, and he drove off breathing a sigh of relief.

Carlos knew the body would be found soon, and he knew eventually the police would track him down, at least to speak with him. He could not deny giving the woman a ride home; the image of them getting into his vehicle in the hospital parking garage and driving away would have been captured on one of the security cameras for certain. He also knew he had to dispose of the knife, still wrapped in the dish towel, and wallet, both of which he had placed in his gym bag. He needed to come up with a plan quickly, and the outline of one began to emerge.

While at work the following day, he spoke with one of the security guards and voiced a concern that he had been followed by someone in the parking garage. He inquired if he would be able to view the security camera footage if for no other reason than to ease his mind. The security guard told Carlos the security videos could be rewound up to twenty-four hours before they were copied to a hard drive and stored, so he was in luck and would be able to review the video right then and there. The guard rewound the video to the point that Carlos and the elderly woman were in picture and then started.

"Wait, right there. Who is that?" Carlos pointed at the monitor, trying to hide the elation that his long shot had come through. A man appeared on the video, walking to his car a few steps behind Carlos.

"Let me see if I can zoom in a little." The security guard maneuvered his mouse and clicked on a few buttons and the picture of the mystery man became clearer. Carlos had to try even harder not to smile as the man's identity became obvious to him. He thanked the befuddled security guard and went on his way.

The man from the video was a hospital orderly named Mika Jackson. Mika was a twenty six-year-old recovering drug addict who had always stood out to Carlos. Despite what he had been told about Mika trying to turn his life around, Carlos always believed him to be a gang member due to his tattoos, and thought he was going to steal drugs or prescription pads.

Carlos was now armed with a plan, and he went about setting it into motion. He picked up his gym bag from his locker and told as many people as he possibly could that he was going to pick something up for lunch and that he might go to the gym. Before leaving, he stopped at the rest room, which he found to be empty. He began rolling out feet upon feet of paper towel from the dispenser on the wall, then took it with him into a toilet stall, shutting the stall door behind him. He rolled up his sleeve and stuffed the paper towel into the toilet until the toilet became clogged. He flushed the toilet repeatedly until it began to overflow, then he quickly exited the restroom and made his way to the maintenance office, which he found to be unlocked with the door open. Carlos entered the office, where he knew the orderlies would congregate from time to time, and found only one sitting at a desk, reading the newspaper. Carlos told the orderly of the flooding toilet and used his smooth talking powers of persuasion to get him to leave the tiny office immediately and tend to the problem.

When he had the office all to himself, Carlos put on a pair of surgical gloves he had in his pocket and retrieved the knife from his bag. He placed it in one of the desk drawers at the bottom of a stack of papers and quickly shut the drawer. Carlos remained in the office and used the telephone on the desk to make a phone call to the management office at the Royal Saxson apartment complex, the complex where his victim lived. He advised he was interested in renting an apartment there but had questions about the security of the complex. He specifically inquired if there were cameras in the parking area or the exterior hallways, and when he was told there were no cameras on the grounds anywhere, he smiled and said he would be in touch and hung up.

Carlos then calmly walked out of the office and went on his way, disposing of the wallet at a gas station near the hospital.

Sure enough, the body of Rebecca Sullivan, Carlos's victim, was discovered by police two days after her demise. He knew it wouldn't be long until the police were able to piece together her last day, and that would bring them straight to him. He began rehearsing his story, preparing to defuse the suspicion he was sure was going to be cast his way. The more he prepared to be interviewed, the more he actually became excited by it rather than nervous. Another challenge; something that got his competitive juices flowing again. It took another two days before a detective came calling at the hospital, looking for Carlos.

The detective had gotten Carlos's name from the oncologist who had requested he speak with Rebecca the day she died. He knew Carlos had gotten in the elevator with her, which was what he told the detective, but that was all he knew, and he certainly did not cast suspicion in Carlos's direction. When the detective spoke with Carlos he had yet to view the security video of Rebecca leaving in Carlos's car, but Carlos didn't try to hide it; he knew that detail would eventually come to light, and so he admitted he had driven her home that day. The detective looked surprised by that admission and began to press Carlos for details, which set Carlos on spinning the deceitful web he had so carefully created.

He told the detective that when the two were walking to his car he felt like he was being followed, but the only person he noticed at the time was a hospital orderly named Mika Jackson, whom he knew and did not suspect. Still, he told the detective, he could not shake the strange feeling. Carlos then told of how he had parked his car and accepted Rebecca's invitation in for a cup of tea. He stated he was inside the apartment for roughly fifteen minutes, describing a surgical procedure Rebecca was to have done and drinking his tea, before he left with her very much alive.

Carlos's gaze drifted from the detective's eyes to a fixed place along the wall of the break room in which the interview was being conducted. He attempted to muster his best look of concern as he told the detective that when he returned to the complex's parking lot and began walking to his car, he noticed Mika sitting in a black Chevy Impala in a parking space with the car still running. Carlos said when he recognized Mika he waved, and Mika rolled down his front driver's side window as Carlos passed. Carlos asked Mika what he was doing at the complex, to which Mika told Carlos he lived there. Carlos told the detective he continued to his car, got in, and drove away without another word being spoken to Mika.

Carlos said he thought nothing of it at the time, assuming Mika did, in fact, live there, but he told the detective that two things had just struck him as odd for the first time. First, why Mika would sit in a parked car, with the engine running, and not go into his apartment? If Mika left the hospital at the same time as Carlos and Rebecca he would have gotten there shortly after they did, so he must have been sitting in his car for a fair amount of time. And second, the look Mika had on his face when he told Carlos he lived at the apartment complex was one of concentration, of determination. It was a focused stare straight ahead, never looking at Carlos as he spoke or passed by.

The detective seemed a bit skeptical of Carlos's story but left him just the same to continue his investigation. Sure enough, as the days and weeks unfolded, Carlos's plan played out just as he had intended it to. Mika was questioned and denied ever being at the apartment or speaking with Carlos at all that day. However, the security video of Mika appearing to be following Rebecca and Carlos out of the building and the word of a respected doctor was enough for detectives to get a search warrant for Mika's apartment, car, and the maintenance office at the hospital. Despite being almost a week after Carlos had planted it, the knife was found in the desk drawer by detectives, and Mika was arrested and charged with first degree murder.

The assumption was that Mika had begun to abuse drugs once again and had stalked Rebecca from the hospital to her apartment, planning to rob her for drug money. After the crime, Mika had panicked and hid the knife at work until he could dispose of it. Mika did have an alibi for the time when Rebecca was murdered. He had gone straight from work to his sister's apartment to try to fix her garbage disposal. However, his sister proved to be of little help to him as she herself was a drug addict with a long criminal history. Her statement was disregarded as one family member, who was unreliable, covering for another.

The trial took a year to conclude, with Carlos involved heavily as the prosecution's star witness. The prosecution did manage to find one other witness, an elderly woman who lived in the same building as Rebecca, stated she saw Mika get out of a black car and walk toward Rebecca's apartment. Her motives for fabricating her story were unknown to Carlos, but he was obviously glad to have her onboard. The apartment complex's manager also testified he received a call the day after the murder from a man inquiring about security cameras on the property. The prosecution then provided phone records to indicate the call had originated from Ft. Lauderdale Hospital, specifically the phone line in the maintenance office. They produced witnesses who testified that Mika was at the hospital during the time the call was placed, and the defense was unable to find anyone who could account for his whereabouts at that moment. The jury took little time convicting Mika of murder, but spared him the death penalty.

Carlos was seen as a hero by the hospital staff. Even people who Mika considered to be friends at the hospital just assumed he had gotten back into drugs and had done it. No one suspected otherwise, least of all that Carlos could have actually been involved somehow, and so the whole thing just went away with Mika's conviction. Everyone eventually forgot about it, except Carlos. Every day since he had committed the murder he would think about it, retracing his steps in his mind. He remembered Rebecca's last moments, her last breaths. He didn't feel remorse or guilt; however, he derived a sense of power from these thoughts. The fact that he had gotten away with it added to his sense of invincibility, his ever growing ego, and the idea that he had superior intelligence. Reliving the murder and cover up in his mind gradually became insufficient, and he knew he wanted desperately to do it again. This time he would be better prepared. This time he would choose someone who could not be traced back to him so easily. And more importantly for him, this time he would take something, a souvenir that would help him to relive his crime over and over again. He would take seven other lives throughout the years. Now he had his ninth victim in sight, and he had no plans on making it his last.

CHAPTER 4

With daylight hours dwindling, a group search for Ashley had commenced, led by Sergeant Stokes. Mike Stokes had been a police officer for twenty years and, at age forty-five, he believed he was about five years from retirement, though he hadn't set an official date. Throughout the years Mike had taken part in several high profile cases and had worn many hats with the department. Cases were always different when they involved children, and this one was already affecting him in ways the others hadn't. Mike had three children of his own: two boys and a girl. Though all his children were older than Ashley, his daughter was his youngest; she was his baby.

He tried to keep himself from making this case personal and putting himself in Tom Wooten's position, but at times he couldn't help it. He thought about how it would change him, as a person and police officer, if this turned out to be a kidnapping. To know that a kind of evil like that existed so close to home was hard for him to swallow. But he was getting ahead of himself. He still couldn't completely kick the feeling she had just wandered off or had gone with a friend or relative and this was just a misunderstanding. As time passed, however, that feeling diminished little by little.

Mike had looked at maps of the immediate area and determined the most likely places a child who wandered off might end up. That was the assumption the search was being conducted under: that Ashley had wandered off. It was too early to predict body dump sites and search them. The problem he faced was that there were no open or wooded areas that a child could get lost in near the gated community the Wootens called home. It was mainly businesses on one side and residences on the other. There weren't a lot of places for her to wander where she would not have already been found and reported, but they pressed on anyway in hopes that they may get lucky.

Based on the police dog's indications of Ashley's direction of travel, Mike organized a modest group of officers, volunteers, and recruits from a current police academy class to search southbound along State Road 441. The road was a major, six-lane roadway that spanned numerous counties and had high volumes of traffic the majority of the time. Mike split his search party into two groups and had one checking the hedges on one side and the second team searching dumpsters, parking lots, stores, and alleyways on the other.

While Mike was organizing and leading his search party, Jim and Dan were back at their desks trying to work on leads or possibilities of who may have taken Ashley. Jim had begun researching the individual who the mall security supervisor had told him was harassing two women the week before Ashley disappeared. His name was Joe Jackson.

On that particular day, the officers who responded to assist mall security with Jackson's departure noted that he smelled and acted as if he had been drinking. The officers spoke with the two women who had reported his harassing behavior, and both said he had followed them for at least a half hour before they reported it. They said he just stared at them without saying anything, but when Jackson was approached by security, merely to ask him if he was all right and if he would stop bothering the two women, he began ranting and unleashed a profanity-laced tirade on the women from afar.

Jim was unfamiliar with Joe Jackson so he began digging into his background for information. Based on his driver's license photo, Joe was a white, possibly Hispanic, man who looked to be clean cut. However, as Jim progressed into unearthing Joe's past, he learned he was anything but.

He had an extensive criminal record dating back to when he was fifteen. Most of the crimes Joe committed at a young age were thefts, but when he turned eighteen they became more violent. Joe had been arrested twice in Fort Lauderdale for robbing and beating two college students who were there on spring break. The charges each time were ultimately dropped for one reason or another. His crimes also progressed to public drunkenness, driving drunk, various drug offenses, and harassment. The one glaring omission from Joe's resume was any type of sex crime or sex offender status, which made him slightly less appealing as a suspect, but wasn't reason to exclude him either.

Unfortunately, the physical evidence that the detectives had to work with at that point was next to nothing. They had no leads other than Jackson, who was iffy at best. They had no vehicle description and only a general direction of travel. There had been no police reports filed in the Wootens' community that would be of any help. Dan printed out a list of sex offenders within a twenty mile radius of the mall and the Wooten home, but unfortunately that list consisted of some two hundred people. The DVDs they had received from mall security would take hours, if not days, to comb through thoroughly.

Word had just gotten back to Jim and Dan that Mike's search party had unearthed nothing of value, which was yet another early blow to their already challenging task. With the odds strongly against them finding Ashley soon, or safe, and with only a limited amount of daylight left, Jim and Dan left their desks and headed out to speak with Joe Jackson.

Tom and Lisa were still out conducting their own search, though they knew in their hearts it was going to be a fruitless endeavor. They, of course, had no idea of where or how to go about looking for Ashley and were simply driving around aimlessly and desperately. Less than eight hours ago the Wooten family was, by all accounts, a typical happy family. Tom ran his computer business, which he had developed eleven years ago. He started out small, purchasing computers in bulk by traveling to estate sales or auctions. Occasionally, in the early goings, Lisa would travel with him and they would make mini-vacations out of the trips, but she had stopped going when Ashley was born. In those early days his business was run from home and the computers he purchased he would repair if needed and resell online. Eventually Tom was able to move his business in to a strip mall in the heart of Boca Raton and he began repairing personal computers as well. He gave customers the option of dropping their computer at his shop or he could come to their homes and fix them there. Even now that he had two full-time employees under him he was still the one to make the house calls to repair computers for customers.

He had always been perceived to be a very nice man, charming, too. He was thought by most to be very handsome and clean cut; an image he enjoyed and worked to maintain.

Tom and Lisa had been together since their freshmen year at Florida Atlantic University. They married shortly after graduation but did not have Ashley until some time after that. After college, Lisa took a job at a local dentist's office as a hygienist; a position she still occupied thirteen years later. She made good money working there and enjoyed her job. It was not as much as Tom brought in, but it was enough to contribute to the Wootens' lifestyle of living comfortably in a beautiful home and a nice community.

Like Tom, Lisa had also aged gracefully throughout the years. Her blonde hair was always done as if she had just walked out of a salon. Her deep blue eyes still sparkled and her smile, which she flashed quite a bit, lit up her face.

And then there was Ashley. Ashley was an only child by choice. They had discussed having another child, possibly more than just one other. But, ultimately they decided one was all they needed to make their family complete.

To those who knew them, the Wootens were the picture of the All-American Family. But now it seemed that picture had been torn to shreds. The portrait of who they were just a short time ago—successful, picturesque, happy, complete—was now gone. They just hoped, as they continued searching down street after street, it wasn't too late to get it back.

CHAPTER 5

Louis was halfway home from his trip to Boca Raton, meandering down back road after back road, going exactly the speed limit. Louis had learned a lot of things while in prison, the utmost prevailing lesson being to limit his interactions with the police. He knew people were after him now: people he had never met or would meet. People he had never wronged or would wrong. He was sure they would look for ways to hurt him, rather than help him, because of what he stood for, because of the title he carried due to his conviction. Sexual Offender. And so he did everything cautiously—including driving.

Prison life was very difficult on Louis. Aside from being an introvert all his life, Louis was branded a pedophile and thus had a target on his back from day one. He was beaten regularly; each time he offered no resistance, just tried to cover his face. He was preyed upon time and time again, just as he had preyed upon his victim. No one had sympathy for him, no one intervened. The only people he could talk to or associate with were other inmates who had been incarcerated for the very same sort of crimes. Never having friends, or even desiring them in his entire life, even that was difficult at first.

When he first went to prison, Louis wasn't sure which way his life would go. He was at a crossroads of sorts. He thought he would eventually get out, although being murdered while serving his time was a real possibility, and at times he thought for sure it was imminent. But still, he wondered what type of life he would have if he did make it through his incarceration. He did not desire the "American Dream" of a wife, kids, or the house with the picket fence. It didn't appeal to him in the least. He had no desire to even leave the safety of his garage apartment he longed so desperately for. What he didn't know was if he would continue down the destructive path that had landed him in his current predicament or if he would work to get past his urges and desires by any means possible. He struggled with this decision for months, until finally he succumbed to the realization that this was who he was. Who he would always be. His urges were a part of him. He wouldn't fight them.

He never felt remorse for what he had done; to the contrary, he felt even stronger now about preying on those who could not defend themselves. He realized that prison would not serve to rehabilitate him as he had been told it would. Prison would serve to sharpen his predatory skills by learning from the mistakes and advice of others.

So over the course of his two years in prison Louis crafted his criminal blueprint. The abuse he took at the hands of those stronger than him only served to make his desire for control more insatiable. When he got out of prison he bided his time. One of the many lessons he learned, and probably the most important, was to be patient. A year passed as he scanned gathering places, learned exit strategies, tested stalking techniques, and honed his chameleon-like appearance. Finally, it was time for him to put his plan into action, and to his surprise it worked perfectly. He would orchestrate it time and again, tweaking it just slightly each time, but never deviating from its core. He was methodical in the completion of his schemes, at times it seemed he was almost on cruise control, but he savored every moment.

Finally, he was back at home from his trip to the mall, having been gone about five hours. He parked the blue Le Sabre as close as he could get to the garage while still being able to swing the door open. He discretely glanced down the driveway to see if anyone was on the street, but noticed no one. He opened the passenger side door, reached inside and scooped up a large quilt from the floorboard. He began to perspire from this brief but strenuous physical activity. He held it in both arms directly in front of his body and leaned his face downward toward the bundle he held tight, his eyes still peering out toward the street. "Don't you say a word," he whispered.

He left the car door ajar as he quickly but calmly entered the garage. Two small white patent leather shoes peeked out from under one end of the quilt and in a flash

Louis placed his cargo, still covered with the quilt, upright and standing behind a stack of boxes. Heavy breathing and whimpers of fear came from under the quilt but Louis paid them no attention.

With his package concealed to any passersby, he calmly walked back to the open car door, reached in and grabbed his police scanner radio off the passenger seat, then shut the door. As he listened during the course of his ride, he was relieved at a noticeable absence in the conversations between police officers and dispatchers. No reference to him, the blue Le Sabre, or his victim had been made once during his trip. However, he knew it had only been forty minutes since he had made his pickup and he needed to get into his apartment quickly to plug the radio back in and ensure the transmission of utmost importance to him was not missed. He pulled the door to the garage shut from the inside and was instantly closed off from the outside world, his captive secured. Just like that.

To anyone who had observed this it would appear as if a man was simply carrying a bundle of clothing. It was so casual. There was no sense of urgency or panic on Louis's part. No sounds were coming from under the patchwork quilt that would have been audible to anyone outside the garage. And now it was over. If anyone had seen it they had already gone on their way not giving it a second thought.

Louis certainly didn't think twice. He never considered his victims' feelings or emotions, and even if he had it wouldn't have mattered much. He had crossed over long ago from simply being numb to being pure evil, with no sense of compassion, only a sense of self. He had blocked out the muffled cries on the trip from Boca Raton to his driveway. They made him feel nothing anyway; transporting was a part of the process, but the end game was the control he felt when he had his victim in his apartment, trapped and looking at him with scared, pleading eyes. As Ashley, no longer cloaked in the patchwork quilt, climbed the ladder to the apartment above with Louis close behind, that feeling finally started building. He was no longer on cruise control.

The transporting, of course, wasn't just a meaningless necessity to Louis. Far from it. It was part of the overall plan, it was a ritual. There was the initial adrenaline rush he got from the actual kidnap itself. That rush came whether or not he was able to obtain his mark, which on many occasions he could not. The patience he learned in prison had been key to his survival thus far, and many times he had to abort his missions because the chance of getting caught was too great. An adrenaline rush with no payoff was very hard for Louis to come down from. Once he crossed over into madness it took a long time for him to come back. Sometimes the rush to abduct his mark was so great that he struggled with the decision to call it off. It was rare that he would be so overcome with his impulses that he acted recklessly and forgot the lessons he learned and rules he had set for himself. Fortunately for Louis, the mistakes he made since his release from prison hadn't been blatant enough to send him back.

Indeed, he had caught a lot of breaks throughout his crime spree; even thinking back to his one and only arrest he had been lucky. He knew he could have served twenty years or more for what he had originally been arrested on, and had his victim and her family not absconded out of fear they would be discovered as illegals and deported, he would have. Of course he didn't know they had fled Davie when he took the plea deal, but he still realized he was fortunate to get such a minimal sentence. He knew that longevity as a criminal of that magnitude didn't come without some luck. He had heard his fellow inmates brag about their successes as well as condemn their failures. Not every crime they committed had been discovered. He knew the tales of Dahmer and Gacy and how they flirted with being uncovered for years prior to their actual arrests. And he also knew some day his luck would run out, just as theirs had.

To keep that from happening any time soon, Louis quite regularly instituted new restrictions upon himself when he felt he was being too careless. He had decided after either a successful or unsuccessful abduction attempt he would not return to the area from which the attempt was made for at least one year, under any circumstances. He also decided that once he was successful and carried out his plan, he would lay low for as long as he could hold out, which at first was extremely difficult. Holding back on acting out was hard for Louis, but over time he disciplined himself and could go six months or more before his demons took over. Thus, in the ten years since his prison release his victims only numbered seven.

But now he had his eighth victim, and she was already in his apartment. The hard part was over. Louis reflected for a moment on how the actual kidnapping wasn't really that hard this time. Things just seemed to play out and open up in his favor. After he pulled out of his parking space at the mall he was able to follow his target with only two cars in between them, and to his good fortune, he was able to remain that way right to the main gate of the complex in which she lived. Again, as luck would have it, there was no security guard at the front gate, and he was able to piggyback his way into the complex.

Once inside, he saw his target make a quick right turn, while the cars between them kept going straight. Louis turned right just as his target was pulling into a driveway on his right hand side. He slowly crept past the house and watched as the car pulled into the garage. He made a U-turn and parked on the opposite side of the street, about four houses down, and watched. He wasn't sure if the opportunity would arise, and he had already accepted the fact that this mission may have to be aborted, when he saw the little girl skip out to the mailbox in front of the house.

When he drove past the house he had seen an empty space in the garage next to where the SUV had pulled in. He made the assumption that another vehicle was generally parked there and was now gone; possibly the girl's father was the driver of the missing vehicle, which would render him absent from the home. As the little girl reached the mailbox the garage door shut. His pulse quickened, his eyes sharpened. He watched the little girl open the mailbox and reach inside and still did not observe her chaperone from the mall anywhere. He also did not see anyone else on the street, though he knew he would have no way of knowing if anyone was watching through a window. He made his move, pulling up next her, where the family's property and the road met.

"Hi, do you remember me?" He said with a smile in a pleasant tone. The little girl turned from the mailbox leaving the small stack of flyers and envelopes inside it. She looked startled, but then she smiled back and nodded her head. "I was wondering if you could help me, I am so lost. What street is this?"

"Palmetto Avenue," Ashley replied in her soft, innocent voice.

"I'm sorry, honey, I can't hear you, I'm an old man. Can you come up to the car and tell me again?" He knew he needed to hurry. Like a viper he was poised, ready to strike.

He could see she had no idea what was in store, she had no way of knowing. She looked at him with familiarity. He knew he had her, if time permitted. She moved up to the car and put her little hands on the open window frame of the driver's side front door. It was over in an instant. Before she even realized what was happening, Louis reached out the window with both hands, adrenaline pumping, grabbed the little girl under the armpits and pulled her into his car, then rolled up the window.

He threw her into the passenger seat and drove purposefully to the community gate. No squealing tires, no revving of the engine, but no dallying either. While he waited for the gate to open and allow him to make his escape, he reached with his right hand and grabbed the shaking girl's shoulder and forced her onto the floorboard in front of the passenger seat. He reached into the backseat of the car and grabbed a large quilt and threw it on top of her.

"Stay there, covered up and I will let you go. I have a gun, if you move, if you make a sound, I will shoot you, then I will go back to your house and shoot your mommy and daddy." His lie subdued the girl and with that the gates opened and he was heading back to Davie.

He reached under his seat and pulled out his old police scanner. The cord had been plugged into an adapter that allowed him to use the car's cigarette lighter to power it. He listened intently, waiting for something to be broadcast about what he had just done. He knew how it all worked by now. The Amber Alerts, the Be-On-The-Lookouts.

He knew where to abandon State Road 441 and how to navigate the lesser traveled roads. Though the demons in his soul were screaming at him to hurry, he meandered slowly, until he made it back safe.

And now he was home, his victim trembling with fear. They were sealed off from the world; she had no avenue of escape. He just sat without speaking, listening to the police scanner. He worried that during the brief time it took him to move it the alert had come out and he had missed it. He sat patiently waiting for it to come, hoping he hadn't.

It had now been over an hour since he had taken the girl. He needed to know what the police knew; he needed to prepare the cover up for what he had done and what he planned to do. But he couldn't wait much longer. His demons wouldn't allow it. That's when he heard a female voice chirp over the radio.

"ATTENTION ALL UNITS. COPY AN AMBER ALERT OUT OF BOCA RATON, PALM BEACH COUNTY. WHITE FEMALE, FIVE YEARS OF AGE, APPROXIMATELY THREE FEET SIX INCHES TALL WITH STRAWBERRY BLONDE HAIR. TAKEN FROM HER HOME IN BOCA RATON AT APPROXIMATELY THIRTEEN-THIRTY HOURS. LAST SEEN WEARING BLUE JEANS, WHITE SHORT SLEEVED SHIRT, AND WHITE SHOES. LAST KNOWN DIRECTION OF TRAVEL WITH SUSPECT WAS SOUTHBOUND ON STATE ROAD 441. NO SUSPECT OR VEHICLE INFORMATION AT THIS TIME. END OF TRANSMISSION."

Louis smiled.

CHAPTER 6

Carlos emerged from his office and proceeded to the living room where Julia sat on a leather couch watching television. "I am off," he said softly as he leaned down and kissed her forehead. Without looking away from the television, she told him to have a good night, and he, in fact, was off.

Julia knew it would be late when Carlos returned, if he even returned at all, which on occasion he did not. He regularly went for late night check-ins with hospital patients or to review files at his office. At least that's what he told her and part of her believed that it was true. She knew him to be a perfectionist and to love his work. She had even brought it up at a Christmas party to the doctor who ran the practice where Carlos worked, Dr. Morris. He confirmed that he routinely found Carlos at the office when he arrived in the morning, fast asleep at his desk with files spread out as if he'd been there all night.

But she also assumed he was having an affair, if not several. He was a very handsome man, always well dressed and very charismatic. He was flirtatious in nature, as well as a highly paid doctor, and so she just assumed at least half of the instances in which he left and was gone all night he was cheating. She never asked him about it though, not once. The truth was she was never really in love with Carlos—only his money and status as a respected surgeon. The more he was gone or secluded in his home office the better. Their sex life was nonexistent, had been that way for years, which was all the more reason she believed him to be having affairs.

Carlos had done well to compartmentalize his life. So had she; she had begun having affairs long ago. It never really mattered to her that she had no solid proof he was doing the same. It never really mattered to her if he was truly having an affair at all, she still would have behaved the same. When he was gone she went out to dance clubs or bars to socialize and have a good time. She would either meet men along the way or, quite often, would go on dates with men she had already met. If, by chance, Carlos came home and she was not there, she would simply say she had been too drunk to drive home and had slept at a girlfriend's house, which he always accepted.

Over the years she had several steady boyfriends, all of whom knew she was married. The sneaking around became an enjoyable part of it for her. She felt covert and intellectually superior to Carlos by doing it. She marveled at how she could outsmart such a well-educated surgeon.

Unlike Julia, however, Carlos was genuinely in love. The only guilt or remorse he ever felt by his actions was that they caused him to be a nonexistent, inattentive husband. He was fully aware of their lack of sexual activity, and even though he found Julia to be extremely attractive and sexy, he simply had no desire to have sex with her. He had no desire to have sex with anyone for that matter. His new release, the only thing that would satisfy him, was killing.

Sexual assault was never a part of Carlos's crimes, however; the sense of control and power he got from taking a life and getting away with it was all the gratification he needed. Nonetheless, he knew his wife needed gratification as well and felt guilty he could not provide it for her. He knew full well that someday his crime spree would end, and when it did and he was exposed for who he truly was it would bring her a great burden to bear.

He had decided about a month prior to this most recent endeavor he was about to engage in to take out an additional life insurance policy on himself. He named her as the sole beneficiary, and in the event of his death she would be set to inherit five million dollars, an amount that would increase by double if he met a violent end. That, of course, was his plan. He decided that if he were ever faced with being arrested and being put on trial he would provoke a "suicide by cop," allowing Julia to collect the insurance money. He had read over his policy several times and, as he understood it, this type of situation would not nullify her payout.

This decision was not an easy one for Carlos to make, in actuality. His legacy was now the body count he left behind. He loved the notoriety he received as the South Florida Strangler. He had studied the most infamous serial killers and wanted to be known as one of them someday when it was all said and done. He knew being unable to give interviews from a prison cell and not having every detail of his horrific criminal activity spelled out in court would hurt that legacy. But he loved Julia so much that he would make the ultimate sacrifice. He was willing to trade the only thing he wanted for his future, the legacy he so desperately craved, for her future. For her forgiveness. However, Carlos had no plans on giving up or getting caught anytime soon.

He drove to a grocery store just inside the Broward County line and parked his car. There was a bus stop outside the store parking lot and he waited with the handful of people to catch the next bus. The store was in a nice area that he regularly drove through to get to work each day and he had no concerns with leaving his car there for as long as he needed to.

He had to dress as he normally would in order to maintain the illusion with Julia that he was going to work, and so he wore tan cotton slacks and a white button down shirt with a floral pattern on it. He had on a nice pair of leather shoes and a three hundred dollar watch, which was his most modest timepiece. Even if he had dressed as casually as possible, he was a neat man to begin with. He knew where he was going to be walking around his attire could make him a potential target. He had been in the area on one occasion—dropping his target off after a consultation. His luxury car had garnered the attention of what seemed like the entire neighborhood then.

The bus dropped him off about two blocks from where he intended to go and he began walking. The streets were dimly lit, and by now darkness had come. He was able to stay on the main road for a fair stretch, which itself was not the safest of streets, but it had higher vehicular traffic and was slightly better lit than the side streets he passed. Finally, he made a right turn onto J Street.

J Street wasn't the worst street in Davie, but it was one of them. It was run by drug dealers and gang members; twenty four hours a day they sat on dilapidated front porches and ruled their court. Sure enough, as Carlos passed by one such front porch, he could hear comments being made by its occupants. He walked faster.

He had done internet searches on J Street and found numerous periodical articles about crimes committed there, however, none of them were homicides, which he found slightly comforting and sort of amusing. He knew this didn't mean none had ever occurred there, just that none had been reported on recently. And he knew if he was successful, which he intended to be, that the most recent such crime to be reported on would have been committed by someone from an upscale, relatively crime-free neighborhood.

Finally, he stood across the street from his soon to be playing field. He used the shadows to his advantage now in case his intended target was to exit the house or look out the window. He noticed no lights on in the main house and checked his watch. The time was only nine o'clock. He knew he would arrive earlier on his "big night" and when he left that evening he would be sure to turn the lights off.

He looked in the driveway and noticed an old blue car pulled so close to the garage door it almost looked as if it had driven right into it from where he was standing. He had not seen this car when he had been there before, but he knew Anne's son lived above the garage and that he had primary use of it. In all his planning and all the planning to come, the son was the biggest wildcard.

It was a situation he had never been in before. He knew it was a huge risk, striking with another resident on the property, but he felt strangely at ease with taking it. All the stories he had heard about this son made him seem like a non-threat. Carlos had confidence that he could complete his task so smoothly that no one would ever be the wiser that he was even in the house until they made the grisly discovery when he was long gone. And if the son did, by chance, enter the main house and discover him there, he would have no choice but to take his life as well.

47

Even Carlos felt it was odd, the strange sense of confidence he had about this particular murder. He had a sense he couldn't fail on this one, even though it provided the greatest chance for him to do so thus far. He began to believe that it was destined to happen; from the minute he chose this victim, he felt something was guiding his hand to her.

As his attention moved from the main house to the garage, Carlos noticed one small window above the door that was covered with very thin, almost see-through curtains. He saw a light on in the apartment but saw no movement. He wanted to stay and continue his surveillance on the son, to see if he emerged at any time from the garage or what time the light went out, but he knew it wouldn't be wise to do so. He could hear people on a porch a few houses away. They were talking about him. He decided he had seen enough to finalize his plan and began walking away.

"Wachu doin out here, homie?" Carlos just wasn't quick enough. A black man, looking to be in his early twenties, had asked the question. Carlos hadn't even noticed the thug approach and he nearly bumped into him as he tried to make his way back to the bus.

"I like that watch . . . those shoes, too. They look like they made out of some fine ass Italian leather or some shit." His gold teeth caught the dim streetlight as he spoke and smiled. His hands were at his chest in fists, flexing the well-defined arms that were completely exposed on either side of his white tank top undershirt.

"So I'm gonna ask you again, what brings a motherfucker with fine shoes like you to this neighborhood?" His jovial tone changed to anger.

For a moment, Carlos paused. His mouth opened slightly and his heart began to race. He tried to focus and steady himself. He looked into the eyes of the young street thug. At first the fear he instantly felt shone through, but then he relaxed. Carlos looked away for a brief moment and noticed that his interrogator was alone on the sidewalk in front of him, but that four of his friends were watching with curious eyes from the porch across the street. He had known this sort of thing could happen. He knew this was

48

the other large risk he would have to contend with. The neighborhood couldn't be predicted. He knew he would have to walk it again. He knew there would be people outside no matter what hour he arrived or left. He knew he would be seen, or possibly worse. It was entirely possible he could be robbed or killed. But, again, he felt confident about dealing with it then. And dealing with it now.

"I think you know why I'm here. Do you have it or not?" There was silence. A look of confusion spread across the face of the street thug, but only momentarily, then a smile returned.

"What are you, a cop? Who told you to come here?"

"I'm no cop and it's not your business who told me to come. I was told this is the place to get the best in town. Maybe I heard wrong. But, as you can tell, I'm not afraid to spend money on what I like. If you can't help me I'll go somewhere else." Carlos started walking away slowly, but felt a strong hand on his right shoulder.

"Hold up, just hold up for a second." The thug looked him up and down. "You got a lot of balls coming here, talking to me like that. I've smoked fools for less. Fact, why don't me and the brothers smoke you right now and take your fine ass shoes and all this money you say you got and call it a day?" He lifted up his dingy wifebeater in the front to expose a black semi-automatic handgun tucked into his waistband. Carlos didn't flinch.

"I suppose you could do that, but then this is all you would get, what I have on me now. I've come to you with a business proposal. I have a thousand dollar a week habit. I have friends who have the same. If this is truly the best in town, as I was told, I'll be back in a few days for more, and so will they. Understand? Don't kill the golden goose, my friend. From what I can tell you don't get many high priced clients."

Confusion again set in on the face of Carlos's adversary. "Yo, I must be trippin," he said in a low tone of voice, shaking his head and causing his dreadlocks to toss about wildly. "Dantrelle, get yo ass over here!"

This was it: Carlos wondered if his plan had worked or if he was about to meet an untimely demise.

"Break this fool off a little something."

"How much you want?" Dantrelle asked in a booming baritone. A hulking black man with a shaved head, he, too, wore a white undershirt that exposed his humungous, tattoo-covered arms.

"A thousand," Carlos said calmly. Carlos took a stack of neatly folded bills out of his pocket and held it in his hand. Dantrelle placed a small baggie of cocaine in the same hand, while simultaneously taking the cash. Dantrelle immediately turned and walked back to the porch without saying a word.

"So what do you and your high places friends do to make all this bank that you spend on blow, anyway?"

"The less you know about me and I know about you the better. This is business."

"Aight, I feel you. I'll be seein you round in a few days then."

With that it was over and Carlos continued on his way back to the bus stop. He breathed a very deep sigh of relief, then he smiled. Yet another boost to his ego, another adrenaline rush that made this upcoming kill so exciting and different. As he turned the corner off of J Street, he took the baggie of cocaine out of his pocket. He untied the twist tie and dumped out the white powder as he walked.

Carlos despised drugs and he rarely drank alcohol anymore. His whole existence was about control—control over others. He would never consider doing something where he would lose control over himself. The way he saw it, a thousand dollars, possibly two thousand, was a fair sum to pay to be able to carry out this particular act. He had the money, and he was fairly certain Julia wouldn't notice if it were missing. He regularly kept at least a thousand in cash on hand, as did she.

Carlos wasn't concerned about being identified by his new friend either, even though he knew he and everyone else on that porch would be questioned after the body was found. But he also knew their house was a drug haven, and all the occupants of it had to be dealers or gang bangers, most of whom probably had outstanding warrants for their arrest. They would not want to draw undue attention to their operation and wouldn't give anything up voluntarily. Nor would they want to give up someone they believed to be one of their most lucrative new clients.

The only problem he saw was if one of them eventually got arrested for something, most likely drugs or some type of violent crime, and wanted to make a deal. But they didn't know his name, where he lived, where he worked, or what he drove. He would dispose of the shoes and watch shortly after the murder was completed, and he knew he had no unique physical features or marks that would assist in identifying him. The way he saw it, the only thing that made him stand out in that neighborhood was that he was so . . . normal.

While Carlos was out laying the foundation for his latest project, Julia was at home, preparing for a night out. She generally only frequented the most exclusive night clubs in Miami or Ft. Lauderdale. She flaunted her sexuality and attracted wealthy men who bought her most anything she wanted. Even though she already had a boyfriend on the side that she had been seeing for four months, she was on her way out looking for more.

She left Carlos the standard cover story note in case he came home, telling him she was out with her girlfriend Vikki and would most likely sleep there.

Carlos sat quietly on the bus engaged in deep thought. It was dark and almost completely empty, giving him the ability to focus. He decided not to go to the office. Instead he would go home and get some sleep. He felt confident in his plan, and the bus ride would be sufficient time for him to hammer out the few details he had yet to diagram. He knew he was set to meet with Anne on Monday to discuss her hip surgery. He felt that he had already won her trust, enough to let him in when she wasn't expecting him, but he knew one more chance to build on their rapport wouldn't hurt either.

He could also attempt to gather more information about her son, specifically his comings and goings and nighttime behavior. Yes, it was decided: he would wait until Monday evening to follow through with his plan. Anne Bradford had less than forty-eight hours to live.

The bus pulled up to his stop and he got off, got into his car, and drove home with a sense of satisfaction. He felt an odd feeling of pride even though he had yet to put his plan into motion. He again felt that this murder was different, like it was destined to happen. He just couldn't shake that feeling. Perhaps it was that he had gotten to know this victim prior to his murdering her, much like his first victim.

Out of all his victims and all his crimes, he thought of his very first victim, Rebecca Sullivan, the least. It was his most unprepared, unskilled crime, and after being as seasoned as he was now, he almost had a sense of embarrassment about it. However, what he did think about, almost more than anything else he had done, was the elaborate cover up he was able to pull off in its aftermath. He relived it again and again.

The fact that he had outsmarted so many and had been able to walk away unscathed was the most gratifying thing he had ever done. What he actually savored was not the kill itself; it was the cat and mouse game he played with police afterwards. It was the terror and fear he was able to inflict upon society, even though he walked in their midst every day. It was the feeling of control that he could stop any moment and no one would ever know it was he who had been the South Florida Strangler.

The South Florida Strangler. At first he didn't care for the name much. He wanted to just be known as himself, Carlos Hernandez, no moniker needed. But he knew that wasn't the way it worked and he knew he had to be given a name for the public to latch on to while his true identity remained a mystery. Carlos knew that the media loved to give catchy titles to criminals. The only ones who didn't get nicknames were the ones whose crimes were not fully revealed until they had been captured. He knew the serial killers and criminals who struck the most fear into the public's hearts and captured the intrigue of many were the ones whose crimes were discovered in real time, and they were the ones given the clever names. The Night Stalker, BTK, the Green River Killer, the Zodiac: they all paralyzed communities with fear prior to their capture. They exhibited the sort of control Carlos wanted, and was now getting.

And so the name South Florida Strangler grew on him. The only thing that bothered him was that he had not gotten credit for his first kill, which he felt he richly deserved. At times he wanted to point out to people in the media that the South Florida Strangler's body count, as they reported it, was off by one. Inside, he demanded his first victim be included and longed to reveal her as one of his own, though he knew he could not. Another man now sat in prison for her killing. Carlos had taken no trophy from her home after committing that crime as he had with the rest. If he was killed resisting arrest, as he planned to be, it would be impossible for police to link her to his other victims.

After the dust had settled on the Rebecca Sullivan case and subsequent trial, Carlos had decided murder was much too messy via gun or knife. There was too much evidence to dispose of and the chance of being caught was far too great. For that reason he decided to strangle his victims.

His second victim was a seventy-two-year-old woman named Elsa McMillan. Carlos had never actually spoken to Elsa like he had with Rebecca, nor had he ever come in contact with her until the day her took her life.

Each surgeon had a drawer for their patient files, which they kept locked while they were away. Carlos had developed a friendship with the majority of the other surgeons employed at the hospital. Regulations on patient confidentiality were less stringent then and many of the surgeons would leave their file drawers unlocked or leave their keys where they were available to other surgeons. Carlos learned each surgeon's upcoming surgery schedules. He learned what types of surgeries were performed, and more importantly, how long the surgeries would take.

If he found himself alone in the office, he would quickly access one of the doctor's drawers and remove the files. He skimmed them until he came across someone who, for whatever reason, struck him. He would dig deeper in that file to see if that particular patient, always female, always

Caucasian, could possibly be a future victim. He tried to choose women as close physically to Rebecca Sullivan as possible. He wanted to relive his first taste of bloodlust. He wanted to perfect it.

After some time passed in reviewing files and choosing candidates, he came across one who seemed to fit perfectly: Elsa McMillan. Elsa slipped while at home in her kitchen and had broken her leg. She had been rushed to the hospital after a neighbor found her after her fall. Her surgery was successfully completed three months prior to Carlos's perusal of her file, and she still made regular visits to have her leg and progress checked. She had originally been taken to a hospital in Miami, however, the doctor that performed her surgery left that hospital shortly after performing it and took a position at Ft. Lauderdale Hospital. Elsa had been made aware of this and insisted upon having the doctor who actually performed the surgery examine her and track her progress, and so she traveled to Ft. Lauderdale for each appointment.

What caught Carlos's eye about Elsa was that she lived alone. It had been noted as the reason why it had taken so long for her to come to the emergency room after she had fallen. Carlos was quick to dismiss anyone as a candidate who lived in gated communities, specifically elderly communities. He knew elderly people in general tended to be more involved in organized or unorganized neighborhood watches.

He staked out his victim and decided it was safe to park his car a few blocks away and walk to her home. He determined the best time to come was during the day, even though the likelihood he'd be seen would be greater. Having never met Elsa, he knew she would be apprehensive about letting him in at night, and his only chance was to come during the day and identify himself as a surgeon at the hospital, which he obviously had the credentials to back up. He would tell her that Dr. Tran, the doctor she had been seeing about her leg surgery, had requested he come and meet with her at home since he knew how difficult it was for her to get around on short notice.

Once inside it didn't take long for his true intentions to show through. Elsa, being more or less immobile due to her injury, was easily overcome and strangled with a pair of pantyhose Carlos had taken from his own wife's closet. The weapon of choice meant nothing to him; he chose pantyhose so they would not immediately puncture the skin significantly when he tightened them around her neck. He was almost gentle when he did it. He simply wrapped the pantyhose around her neck and tightened slowly.

He left Elsa on her living room floor and prepared for his exit. He donned a ball cap, which had been in his back pocket and out of Elsa's view until it was too late. He also put on a pair of sunglasses and a fake mustache, which had been in his shirt pocket. Carlos locked the front door, carefully folded up the pantyhose and placed them in his pants pocket, and then he went to the master bedroom.

He knew he wanted something, some type of visual reminder that he had been there, he just didn't know what. He assumed there would be some trinket in the bedroom that would catch his eye, but to his dismay nothing seemed to do that. He entered the master bathroom, but again nothing seemed to jump out to him—until he opened the medicine cabinet. He smiled when he saw the various pill bottles with her name and address on them. He saw several that had been prescribed by Dr. Tran, but then he saw one that had been prescribed by a doctor he didn't know. He grabbed it and placed it in his pocket. He closed the medicine cabinet, then quickly exited the house from the back.

He was unable to lock the back door as he fled, but he was not awfully concerned about it. He wanted her to be found; he wanted someone to be able to access the home easily. He walked around to the front of the house, fairly confident he had been undetected. He had learned the neighborhood during his reconnaissance missions there. He knew that the neighbors on either side of Elsa, as well as across from her, would be gone to work during the day. The neighborhood was mostly older married couples with grown or no children, however, none appeared old enough for retirement and seemed to go to work each day.

He would do this routine, or a variation of it, again and again, six other times in total. The key to his survival was his preparation and methodical attention to detail. He knew the importance of it and never did anything half-assed. He was not a creature of impulse; he was patient. He did not fear getting caught; his narcissism allowed him to truly believe it was impossible. Even when he transferred to working in private practice he maintained ties to the hospital and was still able to draw from his pool of victims, yet another obstacle he felt very proud of himself for overcoming.

With his confidence in adding to his body count at a high, he pulled into his driveway. He entered an empty, dark house, as he had done many times before. He walked through the foyer, down the hall, and into the kitchen. He picked up a note from the counter:

Went out in Lauderdale with Vikki
Probably staying at her place
See you tomorrow
Love ya, Jules

He smiled and placed the note back down. He felt at peace; he was pleased that his wife was able to go out and have fun and not be resentful of the attention he was not showing her. It eased his guilt for having left her alone yet again.

CHAPTER 7

The annoying chirp of an alarm clock sounded loudly and abruptly. A massive paw quickly slapped it and brought silence back to the dark room. Almost just as quickly, the same hand snapped up a black cell phone that sat next to the alarm on the nightstand. A panicked Jim Brekenridge struggled to focus on the cell phone's tiny screen. The panic was momentarily eased, then replaced with a sense of worry and disappointment. He had no missed calls or messages—the phone only read five a.m.

He set the phone back on the nightstand and sat his large frame upright on the edge of the bed. He leaned his shirtless torso forward as he tried to compose his thoughts and plans for that day. He felt a soft touch on his back and he quickly turned his head around. "Still nothing?" His wife, Jill, asked in a raspy, early morning tone, one eye shut, the other squinting.

"Nope. I thought maybe I missed a call while I slept, but nothing," Jim said as he turned his head away from his wife and looked down at his rotund gut. "Sorry if I woke you."

"No, it's OK, I didn't sleep much either. I don't like seeing you so upset."

"I'm fine. Go back to sleep," he reassured her softly, then stood up and went about preparing for his day.

After dressing in his usual plain white dress shirt, blue tie and tan pants, he kissed Jill on the forehead, grabbed his cell phone, and made his way through the second floor hallway. While he tried to maneuver down the short dark corridor as quietly as possibly, he had the strong urge to glance at his two daughters before he left. Both girls had their doors left open a crack and he peered into one of the rooms and saw his daughter, Lindsay, who always slept on top of the covers no matter what the temperature was in the house. Lindsay was his first born and had recently turned thirteen, a day Jim had been dreading. He smiled, then quietly walked one door to the right and peeked in.

His baby was hard to see, but she was in the tiny bed, covered up to her chin. His youngest, Amy, was six and bore a loose resemblance to Ashley Wooten—at least he thought so.

He turned away from his children's rooms and made his way down the stairs, past the array of photos in frames that lined the wall all the way down. There were various family photos of him, Jill, and the two girls throughout different stages of their lives. Even an old photo of Jim dressed in a University of Miami football uniform, his helmet in his left hand by the facemask, his hair dampened by sweat, his right arm around a very young looking Jill.

The morning commute to work was generally a short one and this morning it seemed particularly short as he was very anxious to get back. He didn't make his usual convenience store stop for coffee and a muffin; instead he decided to settle for the homebrew made in the office to give himself some extra time to run down leads. He generally didn't work Sundays, only a few of the detectives did, though they would all be coming in today.

He was almost certain something would have happened overnight. A tip would come in, a relative would come forward with Ashley and say it was all a misunderstanding. Or worse, a body would be recovered. But there was nothing. He sat down at his desk and pulled out the list of sex offenders Dan had printed for him. Jim would be alone in the office for at least another half hour and he wanted to have some ideas he could kick around with his partner as soon as Dan arrived. So far they had nothing, no real leads, no vehicle descriptions, no suspect descriptions, only the possibility that whoever had taken Ashley had gone south on State Road 441.

The interview he and Dan had with Joe Jackson was fruitless in his opinion, although it didn't officially exclude him as a suspect. They had gone to the address Jackson had listed on his driver's license to find that he no longer lived there, but his mother did. Hesitant at first, Jackson's mother finally gave the detectives his current address, which was an apartment in neighboring Boynton Beach that he shared with his girlfriend and their infant daughter. Jackson was hung over when the detectives arrived and was uneager to indulge their requests for an interview. At first, he refused to let the detectives in and only spoke to them through the door, which, of course, angered Jim.

"Look, Joe, I'm going to be honest with you," he said from the hallway, leaning up against Jackson's door, in the softest, gentlest tone he could bring himself to convey. "We really need you to let us in so we can talk to you. It's up to you if you let us or not, but I can tell you this," his voice began to grow louder and more forceful until he was yelling. "If you don't let us in to talk to you we are going to wait here all day until your baby momma gets home so we can tell her how last weekend you were harassing young girls at the Boca mall!" The sound of the door chain unlocking could be heard, and the door quickly opened, yielding a shirtless, skinny Joe Jackson standing there with one eye shut and one half open.

"Damn man, why you gotta be like that? Come on in I guess." Jim and Dan walked into the apartment, which was small, reeked of cigarette smoke, and had clothes strewn all over the cigarette burn-covered furniture and floor. The entry way opened up into the living room, and Jackson turned his back on the detectives and made his way to a futon. He leaned forward and grabbed a cigarette out of a pack that lay on the coffee table in front of him, lit it, and took a long drag. "Go ahead, sit down, make yourselves comfortable," he said sarcastically.

"I'd rather not," Jim said, his head constantly on a swivel as he approached the coffee table that separated himself and Dan from Jackson. From the living room Jim could see the majority of the kitchen and down a small dark hallway that had three shut doors. "Where were you yesterday?" Jim said turning his attention to Jackson.

"I was here, with my girl."

"All day?"

"All day."

"Here's the thing, Joe. A little girl was taken yesterday. The guy who took her was stalking her at the mall. We know you like to stalk young girls at that very same mall. We know your history. We know you've been escalating. If you did something stupid while you were drunk, now is the time to get in front while you still can."

Jackson's eyes opened wide for the first time since the detectives' arrival. He put the cigarette down in the cut off bottom of a soda can that sat on the coffee table.

"You serious? You think I took a little girl? I *have* a little girl. I ain't down with that shit. There is no way in hell you're gonna pin a kidnapping or some sick shit with a kid on me." Jackson picked up his cigarette, took a drag, then leaned back on the futon shaking his head no.

"All right then, let us look around so we can be sure she's not here."

"Yeah, OK," Jackson said in that same sarcastic tone. "Matter of fact, why don't y'all get the hell out of here anyway. Come in my home and accuse me of taking a little girl."

"Look, genius," Jim said, leaning forward, looking deep into Jackson's eyes. "I don't give a shit about anything else you have going on. I don't give a shit about the bong I see on your kitchen counter. I don't give a shit about the living conditions in this shithole being unfit for a child. I really don't care. I only care about the little girl who was taken. If you don't let me look for her, then I'm going to start caring about all those things and everything else I manage to find in the next few minutes." Jim looked around the living room in an exaggerated fashion.

"All right!" Joe said nervously. "I knew I shouldn't have let you mother fuckers in! Go ahead look around I guess, but I have your word you ain't gonna take me on some stupid drug charge? All you want is to see if the little girl is here?"

"Yeah, sure." Jim walked through the apartment, looking in every room, under every bed, in every closet for any sign of Ashley or that she had at one time been there. He found nothing. "All right, write down who can vouch for your whereabouts yesterday, every second of it." He threw down a small notebook and pen on to the coffee table in front of Jackson. "So help me God, if your alibi doesn't pan out I'm going to be less kind to you next time we speak."

Jim and Dan left the apartment under the same impression they had going in to it, that Joe Jackson had nothing to do with Ashley's disappearance. Dan seemed concerned as they left, however, but it wasn't about his lack of participation in the interview. "You really don't care that two junkies are raising a child in there?" Dan said to Jim as they walked to their car, again calling in to question Jim's tactics in the young investigation.

"Of course I do. We should be able to clear Jackson as a suspect fairly quickly, then I'll contact family services and let them know. If we can't clear him though I want to be able to use that as leverage."

While still waiting for Dan to come in for the morning, Jim sat down and began viewing the mall surveillance video. He tried to focus in on anyone matching Joe Jackson's description, but found no one. He then reviewed the department store surveillance videos and parking lot surveillance videos, and again was unable to match anyone in the vicinity of Lisa and Ashley to Joe Jackson. He officially concluded what he felt he already knew: Joe Jackson did not commit this crime. By this time everyone was coming in to start their day and Dan took a seat at his desk. His desk was pushed up against Jim's in one of the many small clusters that filled the open space of the detective bureau.

"Jackson didn't do it. He's not on any of the security tapes."

Dan turned and looked at his partner's back. "What time did you get here?" he asked, seeming surprised by the amount of work Jim had already done.

"Not too long ago. You got any ideas?"

"Nah, we pretty much knew he wasn't involved. Anything else come up on those videos?"

"Don't know. I just specifically viewed them to look for him. I gotta go back through them or have someone else do it. We need to run down some of these sex offenders, too. In fact, I'll get Bedard to look at these videos; he's got nothing going on. Let's go shake some trees."

Detective Bedard had just walked into the bureau when he heard his name being bellowed out. Paul Bedard very much disliked Jim Brekenridge, but would never admit to it. He had been a detective for five years and had partnered with Jim on a few cases in that time. He was a very non-confrontational, well liked member of the police department, and just went with the flow most of the time. He did not care for Jim's loud, obnoxious, and pushy personality and avoided him at all costs. But he did respect Jim as a detective and had learned a lot from him over the years. Paul took a deep breath and set his car keys gently on his desk, then unenthusiastically walked across the room to Jim's desk.

"What's up? You guys need something?"

"Bedard, we need you to go through these videos and note anyone or anything that looks suspicious. Here," Jim pointed to his computer as he stood up, which displayed the security video from one of the hallways of the mall. The video had been paused and showed Lisa and Ashley fairly clearly. "That's our little girl and her mother. Anyone you see who looks like they are interested in them, note the description and the video's time of day when you saw it. Also, here is a stack of photos I printed from the sex offender registry. If you notice anyone even looking cross-eyed at our girl, try to zoom in on their face and see if they match up to any of them." Jim didn't ask, he told Paul to do all this—he didn't even look Paul in the eyes as he said it. He was too busy gathering his things to leave.

"Uhhh . . . all ri— . . . I mean, I'll have to clear it with the—"

"Thanks, we gotta run. Call me if you see anything important." With that, Jim and Dan left the office leaving Paul still standing at Jim's desk with a look of confusion.

Jim and Dan started by re-canvassing the Wootens' neighborhood to see if anyone had remembered anything and to meet with anyone the original canvass failed to reach. When that yet again produced no useful information, they started a door to door barrage with the people in the county listed as sexual predators and offenders.

At this point they had no real leads and were working more or less blindly. A tip line had been set up and tips were being screened by another detective who would call

Jim or Dan if anything seemed promising, but nothing had thus far.

Hours passed and Jim and Dan continued to get nowhere. Jim tried to sound positive as he spoke with Lisa Wooten on the phone even though he knew they were just spinning their wheels at this point, waiting. Waiting for just one break. For something to go on.

As the pair was getting ready to approach another home, Dan's cell phone rang. Detective Sorrenson, the detective in charge of the tip line, had received a tip from a woman in Broward County that late last night she saw her neighbor in his garage with a little girl. The woman said she knew her neighbor to be a sex offender and that he did not have children of his own, but claimed she was too scared to call right away. It wasn't until this morning that she saw on the news about Ashley's disappearance and the tip line and decided she should call. She gave Detective Sorrenson her neighbor's name and he was able to verify that the man was indeed a registered sex offender. He had been convicted of a sex offense against a child some ten years prior. Dan told Detective Sorrenson to print out a picture of the man and give it to Paul to have him compare it to anyone on the security video. Their first big break in the case sounded promising. Jim's eyes lit up when Dan told him and the two headed back to the station to focus in on their new plan of attack.

The area the caller had spoken of was known to be a very rough part of town. They needed to move quickly but cautiously to ensure not just Ashley's safety, but their own. Jim and Dan worked out the details of their operation with their sergeant, Chris Phillips. Sergeant Chris Phillips was an older man, mid-fifties, who had been a police officer for twenty seven years, a sergeant for fifteen, and a detective sergeant for ten. He was easygoing and generally let his detectives do their own investigations, rarely stepping in or holding them back. In this situation, however, he could not simply nod his head and assume that Jim and Dan would handle things on their own, so he joined in the planning. Finally, after working out the particulars and obtaining a search warrant, Jim and Dan were ready to head to

Broward County, hopeful they would bring Ashley home alive.

Equipped with large bulletproof vests strapped over their shirts with the word POLICE in bold white print written across them, they met with the Broward County Sheriff's Office SWAT commander in a grocery store parking lot several blocks away from their targeted home. Jim had briefed the SWAT commander on the particulars of the case over the phone, so he and his team were prepared when Jim and Dan arrived. They followed behind the SWAT van, which was an unassuming white truck similar to a bread truck on the exterior. When they were at their designated location within view of the home, the SWAT team spread out, setting up a perimeter so that every exit could be observed.

Finally, it was time to move in on the house's occupants. Jim and Dan drew their guns and got in line behind the SWAT team's seven members. They quickly and cautiously approached the house until they were on the front porch, which was so rundown it seemed as if it wouldn't hold them all. One of the SWAT members pounded his fist on the door and yelled for someone to open up for the police. About five seconds later they obliterated the door with a large black metal ram and the SWAT team was inside shouting orders and pointing their guns.

When Jim and Dan made their way into the house, which seemed to be only seconds after the SWAT team had gone in, they observed a woman lying on the floor, facedown, with her hands to her sides and palms facing up. They walked farther into the home and saw a heavyset white male, matching the description given by the neighbor, also lying face down in the same fashion. Two members of the SWAT team remained in the downstairs of the two-story home with Jim and Dan and each had a gun trained on the man and woman. The remaining SWAT members checked the upstairs area of the home for Ashley or anyone else. After several minutes, the entire house was checked and there was no sign of Ashley. Jim leaned down over the man, who was still lying face down on the floor, but at this point had his hands behind his back in handcuffs. "Where's the girl?"

"What girl?" the man shouted back at Jim.

"Where's the girl, asshole? I know she's here."

"I don't know what you're talking about," the man said to Jim as he sobbed.

"Everything clear outside? Can we get into the garage?" Jim bellowed to no one in particular, but got a nod from the SWAT commander in response. The majority of the group moved outside to the unattached garage slowly, ready for their last obstacle.

Jim got ready to pull open the garage door and the SWAT members and Dan raised their guns in preparation for what they may find inside. Jim swiftly pulled the door up and it slid all the way open exposing the inside of the garage. The guns slowly lowered in unison. A stunned silence overcame the group. In the back corner of the garage, under a tarnished yellow bed sheet was the outline of a child sitting down, shaking and whimpering. A large chain stretched from under the sheet to the leg of a large workbench and wrapped around it until it came together at a large silver lock. Jim slowly approached the child, hopeful, yet afraid of what he might find when he lifted the sheet.

He grabbed the sheet with one hand, turned and looked at Dan quickly, then lifted the sheet off. Rarely was he at a loss for what to say or do, but as he stood there, looking at the frightened little girl, he didn't know what to do. Finally, he snapped out of his momentary daze and squatted down next to her. "It's OK, sweetie, we are here to help you. You are safe now." He turned his head. "Someone bring me some bolt cutters!"

Dan had approached by this time and Jim, still squatting, turned to look at him. Jim saw the expression on Dan's face and knew exactly what he was thinking. It was stunned disbelief follow by guilt for what had initially crossed his mind. They had just rescued this poor little girl. They should have felt invigorated, not disappointed. And no doubt they would have, had the little girl been Ashley Wooten.

Her name was Heather Martin and she was eight years old. She had been kidnapped from her home in Texas four months ago. The man who had kidnapped her, who sat in the house handcuffed, held at gunpoint, was named Lee Dixon. He had been arrested for molesting his niece and served five years in prison for it. He bought that home shortly after his release and lived there with his wife, the woman inside the house with him, who he had been married to before he went to prison and who stayed with him throughout his incarceration.

Heather was taken to Ft. Lauderdale Hospital for examination and treatment. The Texas authorities conducting the kidnapping investigation were contacted and were due to arrive in Florida later that night.

The case that Jim and Dan had unwittingly assisted in and helped solve was turned over to the Broward County Sheriff's Office, at least for the moment. The detectives were left to make the drive back to Boca Raton with mixed emotions.

The ride was a silent one, Jim driving, glaring straight ahead at the road, and Dan gazing out the window. Neither knew how to react to what they had just been a part of.

They both felt a sense of deflation and disappointment that they knew would pass. They both knew they would eventually feel a sense of pride for what they had just accomplished. They saved a little girl's life. Heather would have most certainly been killed when Dixon grew tired of her, and until then would have faced daily physical and mental abuse. They knew that the sense of pride that would come with saving Heather's life and putting a violent man away would be that much sweeter if they were also able to find Ashley and bring her to safety.

Jim and Dan were fairly certain Dixon was not responsible for Ashley's disappearance. Heather confirmed that she had never seen another child there, and Dixon's alibi of being at a local hole-in-the-wall bar during the time Ashley was taken was confirmed before they left the town the raid took place in, Hollywood. Before they could cross Dixon off as a suspect they needed to be certain he wasn't on the mall security videos, but they knew he wouldn't be. They were back to no suspects, no evidence, and no leads.

It was late afternoon when Jim and Dan arrived back at the station. Word of their heroic efforts had spread throughout the department, as well as the local news media. Jim knew the Wootens would probably see their involvement on the television or in the newspaper. He knew he should call them to explain what had happened, how things had turned out the way they had. He could imagine how hard it could be for them to see the detectives responsible for finding their daughter finding another missing child instead. He didn't want them to think they were working other cases. He knew seeing the story on the news would be just another reminder that their daughter was still missing, and that good fortune had been bestowed upon someone else, brought about by the people they had hoped would bestow good fortune upon them. Jim stayed behind in the car to call Tom Wooten while Dan went back to his desk.

When he finally arrived back in the bureau, Jim received somber smiles and congratulatory pats on the back, which he ignored. He sat back down at his desk and started shuffling paper around. "Dixon isn't our guy. He wasn't on the videos. Bedard checked each video three times for anyone that might possibly resemble him. Nothing," Dan called out, unprovoked, still looking down at the papers on his desk.

"Yeah, big surprise there," Jim said as he exhaled. "He come up with anyone else on those videos?"

"Yeah, a few people worth looking into. How'd it go with the family?"

"I know you don't have kids, but say you did and one was kidnapped, how would you act?" Jim fired back at Dan.

"Come on man, don't be like that. It was an honest question. Don't be a smartass. I'm upset about this, too, OK? Just because I don't have kids doesn—"

"I'm asking you a serious question so calm down," Jim interrupted, his voice raised. "What would you do, how would you act?"

"I don't know . . . I'd be a mess. I wouldn't be able to do anything but try to find them, why?"

"Even if you weren't a cop, wouldn't you want to be involved in the investigation every step of the way?"

"Of course, yeah, why?"

"I don't know. Tom Wooten wouldn't really speak to me. I called his cell phone and he answered, but when I started explaining things to him he interrupted and gave the phone to his brother. No real explanation for it. If it was me, and my little girl was taken, I would be up that detective's ass every second of every day. This guy sat and waited until crime scene was done to even go look for his kid. I don't know, maybe I'm just fired up still about everything."

"People deal with things differently. You don't think he's involved, do you?"

"Of course not. I mean, at least not directly, no. But I'm starting to wonder if we shouldn't start looking into people with possible motives to hurt him. He's a businessman, has some money, plays golf at a hoity toity country club, handsome guy . . . maybe there's something there. I'm just getting this vibe from him all of a sudden, and it makes me wonder if he isn't keeping something from us. Something he doesn't want people to know about. Something or someone."

CHAPTER 8

Snoring drowned out the sound from the television, which didn't matter much because the only viewer in the room was the one doing the snoring. Louis lay on a worn out plaid upholstered recliner, dressed in a white v-neck t-shirt and black sweatpants. He had been sleeping for hours, gently tucked under a white throw blanket, which had been put on top of him after he had fallen asleep by his mother, just as she used to do when he was a child.

While Louis slept, Anne cooked dinner and tidied up the kitchen. She enjoyed having him in the house, having barely seen him at all over the past two weeks. He had spent the entire day there, which very much pleased and surprised her. She had cooked him breakfast, the two had chatted all morning, and then he stayed for lunch. He had fallen asleep shortly after lunch and had been asleep now for close to four hours.

She knew he was tired; she had heard him start the car and pull out of the driveway earlier that morning. She thought it must have been around three a.m., which was what she recalled seeing on her alarm clock after the car door shutting and engine starting had woken her up. She hadn't heard when he arrived back, but she knew it had to have been after four a.m., which was about the time she figured she got back to sleep.

As her meat sauce neared its completion, Louis stumbled his way into the kitchen, still groggy from his hibernation. He took a seat at the table without saying a word and watched Anne add a few final spices to her sauce. "I hope I didn't wake you," she said as she turned to look at him.

"No, you didn't wake me," he replied, rubbing his eyes. The nap in the recliner was the first sleep he had gotten in almost twenty four hours, but he felt refreshed nonetheless. At some point this became a routine for Louis. When he was done, the wickedness that filled his soul subsided a bit and he would spend time with his mother.

He felt like a different person after one of his acts was through. He felt like his heart had softened a bit and he longed to feel loved. He longed to be doted on and cared for. For a short time he was gentle and meek.

Anne brought the pasta over to the table and made Louis a plate. The two ate and talked some more. Anne, for the first time, revealed to Louis the problems she had been having with her hip and the pain it caused her just to walk throughout the house. Louis didn't even look up, he just twirled spaghetti on to his fork and shoveled it in to his mouth. "Oh that's too bad," he said mid-chew. Anne continued on about her meeting with Dr. Morris and Dr. Hernandez and how they felt she needed surgery to either replace her original hip replacement, or remove some scar tissue that had built up. Louis just watched as his own hand dipped a piece of garlic bread into the meat sauce on his plate, and didn't say a word. Anne, continuing her thought on her hip ailment, told Louis she had another consultation with Dr. Hernandez tomorrow and that she would probably take the car.

Louis stopped eating and finally looked up. Her statement had triggered a rage in him that quickly replaced any feelings of love and pacifism he had harbored. He didn't have to try to conceal his explosive temper or keep up his façade of being normal when he was around her. Although he never became violent with his mother, she had seen the same rage his victims had seen numerous times. "I have to have the car tomorrow! I have plans! You can't just assume you're taking it without talking to me first!" He shouted at her, glaring into her eyes with a look of hatred.

Anne just looked down at her plate and softly apologized and said she would take the bus. She had never been afraid of her son, but she never chose to challenge him on anything he did or the way he treated her either. Anne's husband had passed away when Louis was only five and since then he had been all she had in life. Left with very little money and no family to help her raise him, she always had a feeling of guilt she kept inside for the way his life had turned out. When Louis went into one of his fits of rage she just shrugged it off and tried to move on. She would just let him yell and curse and wait it out until he calmed down, which usually took some time.

"God I can't believe how stupid you are! And selfish! And what the hell is this meat sauce anyway? Is your hip affecting your ability to cook?"

He would carry on insulting her until his blood pressure lowered again, and then he would pretend it never happened. He had never apologized to Anne for anything. He knew she would never hold him accountable, so why should he?

Anne just ate her dinner never looking up at him as he ranted. Despite Louis's disparaging remarks about her homemade pasta dinner, he not only finished his plate, but spooned himself two more helpings.

After the meal ended and his anger had faded, Louis went back to the living room and plopped back down into the recliner. The television was still on and the local news was just beginning. The top story was about a daring police raid in Hollywood that ended in the rescue of a kidnapped girl and the arrest of her abductor. Louis sharpened his focus and turned the volume up. The broadcast detailed how officers from the Boca Raton Police Department had gotten a tip and had worked together with the Broward County Sheriff's Office to raid the house, where they found the little girl chained up in the garage. The attractive brunette reporting the story stood in front of a rundown house that was surrounded by a yellow tape barrier. The woman continued to report the details as pictures of a man and woman who had been arrested in the raid popped up on the screen.

Louis followed the story in amazement. There were so many differences between him and the man who had been arrested, and yet the situation was very similar to what he had just done in so many ways. He couldn't believe it had occurred in the same county. Just a short distance from where he held a little girl captive another man was doing the same.

His mental notes were interrupted by the closing of the news report. "In a bizarre twist, the tip Boca Raton detectives received was not for the Texas abduction case at all," the reporter stated as she looked into the camera. "The tip was believed to be in regards to the disappearance of another missing girl, Ashley Wooten, who was taken from outside her home in Boca Raton yesterday afternoon." Louis's pulse quickened, his face became flush. "All of the officers involved in the raid were under the assumption that she was the little girl being held captive here, and were very surprised to find out that it was actually a different girl. Neither department was aware of the missing Texas girl until after she was located. As for Ashley, police are still very much in the dark as to her whereabouts and who may have taken her."

The screen cut to an older man with gray hair and a gray mustache, dressed in a white shirt and red striped tie, and a subtitle under his picture read "Sgt. Chris Phillips, Boca Raton Police Department."

"At this point we have no real leads on Ashley's whereabouts or her kidnapper. We are asking for the public to help us. If you know anything that may help, please call. Even if you think it's nothing at all, call and let us know. This little girl was doing nothing but getting the mail from the front of her home in the middle of the day when she was taken from her family. We know someone saw something. Please, folks, do the right thing and call in." A phone number flashed across the screen during Sergeant Phillips' impassioned plea. A still picture of Ashley covered the screen, replacing the image of Sergeant Phillips.

Louis, who had been leaning forward in the recliner during the news story, leaned back and propped the recliner's footrest upward. A look of satisfaction crossed his face.

CHAPTER 9

Evening was fast approaching and Jim had no desire to call it a day and go home to his family. Jill had expected as much, and she was fine with it. It very rarely happened, but her husband would occasionally involve himself so deeply in a case that he lost all sense of time. Everything around him became irrelevant except his assigned task, which in this case was finding Ashley.

Jim and Dan had been checking on the Wooten family background for a few hours. Everything seemed normal enough. Both came from good families they remained close to. Tom's brother, Mark, had had his troubles in the past with alcohol and drugs. He had been arrested once for driving drunk, but by all accounts had straightened out his life and now had a family of his own. Lisa had one older sister, Amanda, who lived close by and with whom she was very close, despite the vast difference in their ages. Lisa's sister had two children: a daughter who was in her mid-twenties and lived in North Carolina, and a son, Kurt, who worked for Tom. Tom had hired Kurt as a favor to Amanda seven years ago when he graduated high school. Kurt left his uncle's employ only once since that time, for his freshman semester of college. He returned, however, after learning he had failed out, and he never left home again. He was smart, despite his short lived college career, and he worked hard for Tom.

As far as the immediate family went, alibis would still need to be obtained, but no one stood out as a possible suspect. With that in mind, Jim and Dan decided to speak with work associates first. Dan spoke with Lisa's coworkers at the dentist's office, a small practice, and everyone there had nothing but kind words to say about Lisa and Tom both. The four employees, as well as the dentist, gave no indication that they had any involvement in Ashley's disappearance or knew of anyone who might have. Many of them wept as they spoke with Dan. As for Lisa, they painted her as charismatic and funny, someone who made not only the patients enjoy being there but the staff as well. They all agreed that her family meant the world to her and that she and Tom seemed to have the perfect marriage.

While Dan was talking with Lisa's co-workers, Jim was sitting down with Tom's only other employee, Rick Tardo. Rick Tardo was, simply put, a computer nerd. He had dark black hair, which had always been kept short on the sides and a bit longer than it should have been on the top. His head was very large with his forehead accounting for the majority of it. His brown eyes were covered with large eyeglasses. They looked similar to aviator style sunglasses without the sunglass tint. Black beard stubble covered his ghostly white cheeks and chin despite the fact that he shaved every morning.

Rick admitted to Jim that he had heard of Ashley's disappearance on the news and had tried to get in touch with Tom but was unsuccessful. He was extremely nervous as Jim interviewed him, never once making eye contact, something Jim took note of. Rick explained to Jim the various aspects of his relationship with Tom, both personal and work related. He spoke very highly of Tom, both as a boss and a person. He told Jim that Lisa had always treated him very well and that Ashley always said hello to him when she would come visit her dad. He had even been invited to several barbecues at the Wooten home and the family always seemed very happy together.

Jim began pressing the pedal down. Based solely on body language at that point, he felt like there was a chance Rick could be involved. The fact that Rick was so nervous made an impression on Jim, though he felt confident Rick probably got that way when he spoke with anyone. When Jim finally asked the all-important question of what Rick's alibi was for the time Ashley was taken, Rick, still looking down at the table through his large glasses, seemed surprised.

"Wow, uh . . . I was home all day." He said, raising his eyebrows and opening his eyes wide.

"Why 'wow'? What is 'wow' supposed to mean?" Jim asked in an agitated tone.

"Just surprised you're asking me that. Implying you think I may have been involved."

"Were you?"

"No, and I take offense that you would even suggest it." Rick had a hurt look on his face as he looked down.

"Why won't you look at me, Rick? Are you hiding something?" Jim used a softer voice this time, as if he was trying to coax an admission out of Rick very gently.

"I'm certainly not hiding anything. I'm a non-confrontational person and you're very intimidating." Rick seemed closer and closer to tears with every word.

"Look at me, Rick, look at me," Jim said softly and was finally able to get Rick's eyelevel to rise to his own. "If you did something, now is the time to get in front of it before it's too late. Don't let things go too far to where you can't get out from under what you've done." Rick began sobbing.

"I didn't do anything!" he shouted, his voice cracking as tears filled his eyes. "Tom is one of two friends I've ever had in this world! I would never do that to him!" Rick sniffed hard and took a deep breath. "That little girl was his world. He loved her more than anything. He hated going on so many repair calls late at night because he missed spending time with her. She was a nice little girl, always said hello to me. Most people who see me dismiss me or laugh at me because of how I look or how I act. She was nice to me. They all were nice to me." He began uncontrollably weeping. Jim looked down at his watch for the first time all day. He was genuinely surprised that it read seven-twenty p.m. He knew he was due home over two hours ago and there were still a few things he wanted to do before he left for the day.

"OK, Rick, before I go, would you mind allowing me to look through your room real quick?"

"Why?" Rick asked as the tears began to subside.

"Why?" Jim replied back, the soft, gentile tone was gone from his voice. "Why do you think? If you want me to exclude you as a suspect I need to make sure Ashley isn't here now and has never been here." Rick paused as he again looked down at the table.

"I just don't understa—" Rick's words were interrupted by Jim's cell phone ringing.

"Hold that thought." Jim said as he pulled the cell phone out of his pocket and answered it. Almost immediately his face turned ashen. His heart sank. He could barely muster enough of his voice to reply to the person on the other end that he would be right there. He slowly raised himself from the seat at the kitchen table, looking dazed. Rick looked up at him confused and scared. "We will have to continue this later," Jim said in a tone that was barely recognizable to either of them. Jim exited the house the way he had come in.

Where he was headed wasn't a very long drive, but it seemed that way. Jim had the car am/fm radio turned off and just listened to his own inner monologue the entire way. He played out several different scenarios in his mind and what he would do if each one of them came up. Finally he arrived at the location Sergeant Phillips had described and parked on the side of the road behind an array of police cars, both marked and unmarked. He scaled a guardrail with relative ease and began his slow descent down the side of the hill toward the group of police personnel that were gathered on the side of a canal.

Florida was riddled with small canals and waterways throughout the state, and Palm Beach County was no different. This particular canal was rather large, roughly fifty yards across, and was right on the border of Palm Beach and Broward County. Roads paralleled it on either side, however, the Broward county side had virtually no houses near it and the road that ran beside it was much less traveled. The roads on either side of the canal were raised, with a rusted guardrail separating the blacktop, in some places dirt, from a twenty foot sloped decline to the canal.

Jim cautiously approached the group of police officers and crime scene techs that formed a semi-circle from the water's edge. The group consisted of four uniformed Broward County Sherriff's deputies, two men in suits Jim didn't recognize, Dan, Sergeant Phillips, and several crime scene technicians from Broward County. He knew what he was about to see—he had known he would most likely see it at some point from the minute he realized he was working a legitimate abduction—he just had hoped he wouldn't. He knew he needed to brace himself for an image that he would most likely remember for the rest of his life.

The group still stood in a semi-circle, backs turned to Jim when he placed his hand on Dan's shoulder. Dan turned around with a look of disappointment and sorrow, then stepped aside and let his partner in on the discovery. Jim let out a deep breath and began inspecting.

Strawberry blonde hair lay tangled and uncombed as it partially covered her shoulders and her forehead. The collar of her white shirt was flipped up, the three small buttons unbuttoned. The front of the shirt remained mostly white, but mud stains from the back protruded from both of her sides. Dampness covered the bottom of the shirt from her belly button down, as well as her back. Her blue jeans were buttoned and intact, however, they were soaked from front to back and covered in mud. Her right foot was exposed, and her left was covered by a shoe. A patent leather shoe, that at one time was white, but now was stained by mud. Her milky white skin still looked like that of a porcelain doll, but mud spots and blades of grass dulled it slightly. Her eyes were closed and if it wasn't for a large red line going around her neck she would have appeared to have been napping right there on the grass.

No one said a word as Jim took in the heartbreaking sight. He had only seen her in one picture before, but as he looked at her now he knew she must have been so full of life only a short time ago, such a bright light. Her skin, her hair, everything about her just seemed faded. The few white areas left on her shirt and shoes seemed brilliant in comparison. The grass beneath and around her seemed so bright green. He thought of the point in the movie *The Wizard of Oz* when the screen bursts with color from what had been just gray, dull imagery. Everything around her seemed to burst with color, to burst with life, while she remained gray.

Jim began to slowly accept what he was seeing and get past the sorrow he felt in his heart for a little girl who would remain frozen in time at the age of five. He started gathering facts on how Ashley's body was discovered and anything else that would be useful to the case, which had suddenly gone from a kidnapping to a homicide. Jim was told that roughly an hour before he arrived the sheriff's office had received a 9-1-1 call about a little girl's body being found on the bank of the canal, partially submerged in the water. The caller seemed shaken but certain it was "the little girl who was missing" and urged the dispatcher to send someone quickly, then abruptly hung up.

Two deputies arrived shortly after the call was received and found Ashley's body. She was lying on her back, much like she was when Jim saw her. However, her lower torso was submerged in water up to just above her belly button, and the deputies made the decision to carefully pull her back out of and away from the water.

Jim was directed to the caller, who he had passed as he walked along the bank on his way to Ashley's body but never noticed. He was an older, short, heavyset black man wearing dirty blue jeans and a white short sleeved t-shirt. He sat on the hillside holding a fishing pole in one hand and a black tackle box in the other. The man's name was William Henderson. He told Jim that he fished the canal often, several times every week. He said he hadn't noticed the body when he first arrived, even though he was fishing only a couple hundred feet from it.

After being there for about a half hour he decided to walk down the canal a bit to try to find a better spot, and that was when he saw Ashley. His voice cracked as he spoke. William said he ran to the little girl and recognized her face immediately. He said he lived in Boca Raton and had seen the news story on her abduction. He checked for a pulse but he couldn't find one. William told Jim he wasn't even sure if he had done it right, but that her skin was cold and her body was lifeless and he just had a feeling she was dead. William said he panicked after that conclusion entered his mind. He ran to his tackle box and retrieved his cell phone and placed his 9-1-1 call.

"I didn't know what to do, I didn't know if I should pull her out, I didn't know . . . I didn't know," he wept. "Please tell me I couldn't have saved her. Oh Lord, please tell me that."

"You couldn't have saved her, sir. You did your best." In a time of great agitation for Jim, this was a rare moment of compassion. He didn't allow his compassion to linger, however, as he quickly requested William's address and phone number in case a follow up interview was needed.

"I don't know how the gators didn't take her," he said as he wrote his information on Jim's notebook paper. His voice was a bit sturdier and calmer now. "They out here, all over the place. Sometimes I have to drop my pole and get back cause I afraid they gonna jump out the water and snap at me. It was like God wanted someone to find her. Like God wanted her to be brought back to her parents. There really is no reason why a gator wouldn't have taken her, 'cept for God."

Jim returned to Ashley's location where Dan and Sergeant Phillips still stood. "We have to tell the family. The media is going to be all over this soon," he said to both of them.

"Yeah, you better get going. Broward isn't going to give us any problems on this one. They said they will assist with the investigation as needed and that their crime scene will report directly to us. We are going to have to use the Broward M.E. though and they will be taking the body to their headquarters," Sergeant Phillips said as he continued to look down at Ashley.

"Are you kidding me? These poor people lost their only child and now we are making them drive all the way to Ft. Lauderdale to identify the body? Come on, Chris, that's ridiculous." Jim looked into Sergeant Phillips's eyes, even though they didn't return the glance.

"I know, I know, but what can we do? It's a jurisdictional thing, you know that. Procedural. Now you guys need to get going before that news chopper starts flying over." Sergeant Phillips took a deep breath. "God, it's fuckin terrible," he said as he exhaled and looked up at the water.

Jim took one last look at Ashley. The image of his daughter, Amy, superimposed upon her. His thoughts began to head in that direction. What would he do if it were his child? Could he cope with the pain and suffering it would bring him? He quickly cast the thoughts aside and began making his way back up the hill, with Dan close behind.

Ashley's body had been located on the Broward County side of the canal, making the homicide investigation, at least initially, the responsibility of the Broward County

Sherriff's Office. However, Ashley's abduction had been news across South Florida and so the deputies who first arrived at the canal were able to quickly identify the body as Ashley's.

Jim and Dan had driven separately to the canal, and thus they had to drive separately to the Wooten home. Both were affected not just by Ashley's death, but by physically seeing her dead body. Both had seen dead bodies before on numerous occasions in their careers. They had both been unlucky enough to have seen dead children before, on one occasion each, and it was something that affected them both and was impossible to forget. The children they had seen, however, were victims of a car accident and a drowning. One had physical signs of injury far worse than the few that Ashley had. In those cases, however, there was no before and after. There was no race to save the child. There was never any hope, no matter how slim, that the child may turn out all right. There was only the after, there was only death.

They had an investment in Ashley Wooten, and now they had to change gears from trying to rescue her, as they had rescued Heather Martin, to trying to bring to justice her captor and killer.

Heather Martin. Suddenly that seemed so long ago, though it had only been a little over five hours since they watched her climb into the back of an ambulance and be driven away. They had had mixed emotions at that time as they drove back to Boca Raton, but they both had hoped they could fully celebrate the good they had done when they were able to bring Ashley home. And even though they were bringing her home in a way now, they knew any celebrating or feeling of a job well done would be a long way off.

Both Jim and Dan would have preferred a longer drive to the Wooten home. The news they were bringing wasn't pleasant by any means, and neither wanted to give it. Dan knew it would be Jim who would ultimately break the news to the family, and he was both relieved to know this and worried about his partner.

Even though he couldn't relate to the love a parent felt for their child, Dan still knew breaking the news would be hard and that he would have to be strong in doing so. He had done death notifications before, but felt this one would be different given the circumstances. As a police officer, he was the image of strength, of reassurance. If he broke down the perception might be that this horrible thing had overcome everyone and there would be no one to be strong, to try to find answers, to try to find justice.

And in all honesty, Dan didn't know if he would be able to be that person. He was confident he could be if he didn't have to give the initial news, if he could stand by and at a later time offer condolences. That seemed different to him. But he was fairly certain he would stammer getting the news out, and it was possible his voice would quiver and crack. He knew Jim wouldn't have these issues. Though at times Dan did not enjoy being Jim's partner because he felt shut out by Jim's domineering nature, in times like these he was glad Jim was his partner for the very same reason.

It was dark by the time Jim and Dan caravanned into the gated community where the Wootens lived. Jim had phoned Tom while he drove to let him know they would be stopping by to speak with them. Tom just acknowledged Jim's statement and told him that when they arrived at the gate to dial the numbers one, one, zero, then six into the callbox and the gates would open. Jim again noted to himself Tom's lack of questions and his seeming reluctance to engage in conversation, however, he also noted Tom's voice had a worried tone to it.

Jim pulled up in front of the house first, with Dan right behind him. There were two cars in the driveway that Jim did not recall seeing the day before when they had been at the Wooten home. He assumed family members had come to stay with the Wootens, which made what he was about to do both easier and harder at the same time. He would have the assistance of loved ones in comforting Tom and Lisa after he broke the tragic news to them. However, he would also have the burden of having an audience for his notification. Loss made people react in funny ways and the more people that would have to deal with the news of a loss, the more possibilities of someone dealing with it violently. But there was nothing he or Dan could do about that now, and they both gave each other a look as they stood at the front door as if to indicate "this is it."

Jim rang the doorbell and heard a scramble coming from inside. The door quickly opened and Lisa stood before him. Her eyes were red and puffy. Her hair was uncombed. "Hello," she said in a soft tone, then sniffled. "Come in, please."

Though she tried not to make it obvious, she peered behind the detectives as they entered the home, as if maybe Ashley was hiding behind them and they were playing a trick on her. At any moment they would shout "SURPRISE" and Ashley would run into the room and jump into her arms. But of course there was no one else with the detectives, no one waiting just outside for a cue to come in, and so she shut the door.

Jim and Dan stopped a few feet inside the home in the foyer area. Family members gathered around them, much as Jim and Dan had gathered around Ashley just a short time ago. Tom stood by Lisa. To the left of Tom was his brother, Mark. Standing behind Lisa were her parents. They all looked at Jim as if they couldn't breathe until he spoke. As if the words that would come out of his mouth were vital to their existence. As if they already knew what was coming but had to hear it anyway. Jim looked into Tom's eyes, then he looked into Lisa's. He saw a look of fear. He summoned courage from deep inside him and widened his gaze to include them both.

"I'm sorry to have to tell you this; your daughter has been located. She's dead."

Ringing filled Tom's ears. The back of his neck and face burned. The room was silent. No one was there. He was suddenly blinded by liquid filling his eyes and blocking his sight. What was only a second seemed like an eternity. His mind was blank, he felt no emotion, he just stood. Then, with his eyelids acting as windshield wipers, his sight returned. The screams and chaos that had filled the room suddenly hit his ears. He felt his brother pull him close and wrap him in an embrace. Was this real? What was happening here? Finally, his mind snapped back to reality and began to focus in on what was happening. His daughter was dead. His heart, his soul, his life, all gone.

He would never again touch her soft skin. He would never stroke her hair, he would never kiss her forehead, and he would never hear her sweet voice say the words "Daddy" again. Though he had been crying as almost an instinctual reaction upon hearing the news, he now understood why and began sobbing harder as he wrapped his arms around his brother and squeezed.

Lisa had collapsed to the floor upon hearing the news. She repeated the word "no" over and over as she cried. Her mother, who was also sobbing uncontrollably, knelt beside her and tried her best to comfort Lisa through her own tears. Lisa's father, a crusty former marine and retired auto mechanic named John Harmon, looked around. Tears ran down his cheeks. He looked at Jim and took several short breaths as if he wanted to say something but was having a hard time getting the words out. Finally, he took a step closer to Jim and said quietly, "I'm sorry, I know this must have been a hard thing for you to do." The man's chin began to quiver after speaking. As much as he had tried to compose himself he was starting to come undone and so he quickly turned away from everyone and walked down the hall and into the kitchen.

Jim stood quietly, fighting his own emotions. He was close to losing his composure but was managing to keep it together. He knew he had to get out of the house. He needed to leave, to be alone. He feared that hearing a man who had just lost his granddaughter, who watched as his daughter lay on her own hardwood floor weeping uncontrollably, tell him that he felt badly for the emotions he knew he was feeling would push him over the edge.

Tom was able to gain enough composure to pull himself away from his brother and turn back toward Jim. Still visibly crying, he asked the obvious question of how. How did she die? He spoke in a low voice, very soft, as if he could muster no higher volume. Lisa continued crying and did not look up from her location on the floor. Jim wasn't sure if she had heard her husband ask the question and he really did not want to have to repeat the answer, so he paused a moment before responding. Lisa's father re-entered the room and awaited Jim's response. Jim cleared his throat and regrouped. He was composed again; he was prepared to answer the questions he knew were coming in a factual, straightforward way.

"She was strangled." Tom gasped and put both hands on top of his head. Mark put his head down and cried. Lisa's father began breathing heavily as he leaned against the wall. His breathing was noticeable, loud, and deliberate. Jim looked at him in fear he was having a heart attack. "Are you OK, sir?" He asked, afraid the family would have another tragedy to deal with. Just then Lisa's father spun around and punched a fist sized hole in the drywall while letting out a grunt. He then placed both hands on either side of the hole he had just made and hung his head, catching his breath.

If Lisa had not heard Tom's question, she apparently heard the answer. She vomited all over the wood flooring where she knelt on her hands and knees. Tom started again, trying to ignore his wife's cries.

"Where, uh . . . did you find her?"

"She was found along the bank of a canal not too far from here, the one along the Broward County line." Jim said very matter of factly. Tom nodded as he wept as if to say he understood.

John, still breathing heavily, had turned away from the wall and again approached Jim. This time, however, he seemed less than cordial.

"Who did this?" he shouted. "Are you going to catch him? This sonofabitch, this sick bastard, are you going to catch him?" John's eyes were on fire as he shouted at Jim. The comfort he tried to bestow on Jim earlier was gone; now he wanted answers.

"We will get him, I can assure you. We won't stop until we do. I want this guy just as bad as you do, trust me." Normally had anyone talked to Jim like that he would have been incensed, however, he understood the circumstances and he spoke in a very calm and reassuring tone. John nodded his head in acknowledgement and walked back in to the kitchen.

"What happens now? I mean . . . when can we . . . get her or . . . I'm sorry," Tom asked through his tears, not acknowledging his father-in-law's short tirade.

"I know this is hard, folks, and I want to give you some space, so I'm just going to tell you what we know as opposed to making you ask me. I don't mean to sound cruel or callus, but I'm just going to tell you everything at once. Your daughter was abducted by someone, we don't know who, and then she was most likely laid along the canal after she passed. We don't know much else at this point, but she was completely clothed when she was found if that's any consolation. A fisherman found her about two hours ago and called us."

He paused, then proceeded, "she will have to have an autopsy done before you can have her taken to a funeral home." He paused again. He knew that was news people don't generally think of or like to hear, and this was no exception. Tom closed his eyes hard. "Someone will be in touch when that has been completed. Unfortunately, her body was found in Broward County, which means it was taken to the Broward County Medical Examiner's Office in Ft. Lauderdale. We will need you to come identify the body as hers."

"Tonight? Is that really necessary right now? I mean, jeez," Mark shouted at Jim.

"No, it doesn't have to be tonight. It can be tomorrow morning, and we don't need both parents, only one will do, it's up to you." Jim responded very calmly. Lisa stopped crying and stood up. She approached Jim and stood within inches of him. She looked up at him as he looked down at her, not sure what had caused her sudden composure and what was coming next.

"So, you mean, there's a chance this isn't her? I mean, if you knew it was her, you wouldn't need us to identify her. We could go there and it could not be her. Or we could just not go there at all and—"

"I'm sorry," Jim interrupted, "but from the picture you gave us we are certain it's her. It's a formality really. I didn't mean to mislead you."

Lisa erupted in to tears again.

After a few more reassuring words, Jim and Dan made their way out the front door and to their cars. They both agreed it was time to head home and that they would see each other in the morning. Jim was quick to pull away from the house. The death notification was just as difficult as seeing a little girl robbed of life. He began driving home but, although he could escape the Wooten home, he could not escape his thoughts. He couldn't get past John wishing him his condolences. It was heartbreaking to think about. He could feel tears welling up in his eyes. For the first time he wept for Ashley. He wept for her family. And then he inevitably placed himself in their position and wept for his daughters. He longed to get home to them, to touch their skin, to kiss them, to hug them, to tell them he loved them and to make sure they were real.

He pulled into his driveway and sat in the car for a minute to calm himself down. He took several deep breaths and thought of things that he hoped would calm him. Baseball. Who were the Marlins playing tonight? They had been rolling as of late; of course he hadn't seen a game in two days. He seemed calmer now, relaxed enough to go into his home and spend some time with his family. As he walked through the front door he saw his oldest daughter, Lindsay, lying on her stomach on the living room floor, both hands under her chin, elbows on the rug, watching television.

"Hi, Daddy," she said without looking up.

"Hi, baby," he said as he looked down at her lovingly.

He stopped and continued his gaze for a moment. His eyes displayed a mix of love and sadness, his lips pursed together. Jill had walked around the corner from the kitchen and stopped as she saw the look on her husband's face. She knew. She hadn't watched the news all night, even though she had tried to remind herself to. She had no idea about the child her husband had helped save and the child he discovered he could not. When she saw his face she realized the latter had occurred. Jim looked up at her and followed her back into the kitchen. As soon as they were out of view of Lindsay she gave him a spirited embrace.

"I'm so sorry. You did what you could," she said even though he had yet to confirm what she believed she knew.

Jim shrugged. "Thanks for letting the girls stay up so I could see them, I needed it. It's been a crazy day. I've never had a day like this before. Hope I never do again." Jim proceeded to tell Jill everything that had happened since the time he walked out of the house earlier that morning, the good and the bad.

Jill cried tears of joy and pride as he told her about Heather. She cried tears of sadness when he told her about discovering Ashley's body and delivering the news to her family.

"You're a hero. You're a strong man. You saved a little girl's life today and now you'll fight for another little girl who was taken from her family. I love you." She hugged him again. Just then Amy wandered into the kitchen looking for a snack. It didn't take her long to realize her mommy and daddy were upset and she began asking questions as to why.

Jim reached down and scooped her up into his arms. "I just missed you so much today it made me sad," he said as he pulled her close. She seemed to accept this answer and laid her head on his shoulder. He closed his eyes as he held her and, though he wasn't a religious man, he said a little prayer thanking God for the safety of his family.

Then, as he held her close, a new emotion overcame him. To this point he had only felt sorrow, but now he was suddenly overcome with rage. He could feel anger building inside him. Who could hurt an innocent child like that? He couldn't imagine the type of person that would do such a thing to a beautiful child, much like the one he was holding in his arms and treasured more than anything.

He put Amy down and walked back toward the front door and opened a door next to it, which led into his garage. He shut the door behind him and flipped on the light. His garage was cluttered with various tools and lawn care items. It also housed one of the family's two cars and a washing machine and dryer. Jim placed both hands on the washing machine and leaned forward, hanging his head. His breathing became quicker and quicker through his nostrils as his anger began taking over.

As strange as it sounded, he hadn't really concentrated on the person who had taken Ashley up to that point. Obviously, all the work he had done up so far was trying to discover the person's identity, and he knew he would be dealing with someone he'd despise, but his main goal had been to find Ashley, safe, and bring her back to her family. Now that he would not have the chance to do that he wanted the person responsible for her kidnapping and murder to pay for what he had done. He wanted the person responsible to be punished, severely. In this moment he wanted it badly. He wanted to inflict pain on this person, this animal.

A hatred began brewing more so than he had felt before. He hated this person, this ghost he was now chasing, not just for taking the life of an innocent child and ruining a family, but for how this person had affected him in doing so. He would never get the image of Ashley's body lying on the grass by the water out of his head. The image of her neck, red and indented by the cause of her demise. He turned and stood erect. He desperately searched for something to punch. He needed to somehow release this anger. He raised his right fist and took aim at the wall.

"Don't you dare!" Jill shrieked at him as she burst through the door. He turned and looked at her; his eyes still radiated hatred and anger. She quickly shut the door behind her and ran to hug him. He lowered his fist and closed his eyes, hugging her back.

Jim received a call around seven the following morning from Tom's brother, Mark. Tom and Lisa were ready to identify the body and wanted to get it over with as quickly as possible. Jim and Dan met the Wootens, including Mark, in front of the Broward County Medical Examiner's building at eight a.m. Tom and Lisa had gotten no sleep all night and Jim had gotten only slightly more than that. Both Tom and Lisa had red, puffy eyes as if they had not stopped crying since the detectives had seen them last. They seemed absent, as if they were just there physically, nothing more. Mark had slept on the couch last night, and planned on doing so all week. His wife and kids were going to come by and bring dinner later that evening. He had cleared it with his boss to miss at least a week of work, if not longer.

Mark and Tom had always had a good relationship growing up, maintaining it throughout their lives. Despite Tom's successes and Mark's struggles, Mark never resented his brother; in fact, he looked up to Tom. But now Mark was the one being called upon to be stable. He was the family head now, he was making the decisions Tom and Lisa needed to make. He was taking care of them both with whatever they needed to make them feel slightly better or less encumbered. He was strong while they were paralyzed with sorrow. But inside he was hurting, too.

He had lost a niece, a little girl he had known and loved since her birth. His children had lost a cousin and he knew he would have to tell them later that day, which agonized him. Mark felt like he owed this to Tom; he felt like now it was his time to step up, to be the brother that Tom had always been to him. It was important to him. He had rarely seen Tom upset before and never to the extent he was now. As much as he dismissed the thought that seeing his brother in such a state was affecting him the most, it was probably true.

Lisa's parents had gone home about two hours after Jim had broken the news of Ashley's death. Lisa's father ended up in the emergency room at three a.m. after breaking his hand from that punch to the wall. A boxer's fracture of the knuckle area. Nevertheless, they were planning on coming back later that day. Lisa's sister had also made arrangements to be off of work and would check in on them at some point. Tom and Mark's parents had been told the horrifying news over the phone by Mark and they had planned to arrive at the Wooten home that day as well. An insulated layer was forming around the family, but Lisa and Tom couldn't really appreciate it yet.

"This is going to be difficult," Dan said, speaking up before Jim had a chance to. "Take as much or as little time as you like. You will be on one side of a window. Your daughter will be on the other. When you're ready, I will tap on the glass and the shades will go up. You will see her. You don't have to say a word, a nod is good enough. Unfortunately, you won't be able to be on the same side of the window as she is, but you will have time to see her and touch her when she arrives at the funeral home." Dan placed his hand on Tom's shoulder. "Let's go," he said and walked into the building.

Finally, the group arrived at the window. The shades were drawn. Tom and Lisa stood before it, Tom with his arm around Lisa's waist. Lisa had begun crying again as Dan spoke but she tried to compose herself as they reached their destination. Dan stood to the right of them against the glass. He stared at Tom and Lisa, waiting for the signal. Jim stood behind Dan, also keeping a watchful eye on the Wootens so he could be prepared for what followed.

Tom swallowed hard. He could feel his heart racing. His breathing deepened. This is it, he thought to himself. It's real after this. My eyes can never unsee what's on the other side of this window. "Are you sure you want to see this?" he asked Lisa.

"Of course," she said back to him through her sniffles. Tom looked at Dan and nodded.

CHAPTER 10

Only two raspberry cream filled donuts remained in one of the four boxes on the counter. That had pretty much been the case every Monday for about a year. No one seemed to like the raspberry cream variety, except the person who ordered and picked up the donuts, and thus, their inclusion in the four dozen continued. Why he got so many, however, would forever be a mystery. The coffee line had dwindled to only two men dressed in black suits, with everyone else in the large conference room having taken a seat at one of the numerous long tables. With the final two members of the group having filled their coffee mugs, the meeting was set to begin. Three large white dry erase boards with various messages scribbled across them stood in the front of the room near a podium. A long table, similar to those currently occupied by the meeting's participants, was covered in boxes, files, and pictures.

A man entered the room and walked to the podium. He had short gray hair that was combed back on the sides and parted on the right side of the top of his head. Despite his age, fifty five, he looked to be in good shape. His face remained chiseled and tight, no sagging skin or double chin. His suit was black in color and looked like it had just been taken from the cleaner's rack. His shirt was blue; his tie was blue with red stripes and tucked neatly under the buttons of his jacket. He adjusted the microphone on the podium out of his way and looked out into the group of twenty men and seven women.

"All right, folks, let's get started here. I hope everyone enjoyed their weekend. Thankfully we weren't called in for anything, so there is nothing really new to report. It's now been a little over six months since we've heard from our guy. That's a long time for him to go. He has never gone that long in between kills in the past, and, if he is still able, I wouldn't expect him to go much longer." He spoke as if he were reading off a script, as a news anchor would, although he had none in front of him. He was an excellent public speaker, and had been an excellent police officer his entire thirty year career. Which was precisely the reason the sheriff had put him in charge of the South Florida Strangler taskforce.

The taskforce had been formed a little over a year ago, after it was discovered there was a serial killer at work in Broward and Miami-Dade counties. A discovery that stemmed from the diligent work of a Pembroke Pines Detective named Jorge Salazar.

He was working the homicide of an elderly woman named Tanya Moore about eighteen months ago. She had been found in her home, strangled to death. As part of his investigation in to her death, Jorge was checking Tanya's phone records and bank statements when he discovered that she had been in contact with a personal injury attorney named Pete Rubino regularly for the two years before her death. She called him or he called her approximately once a week and they would speak for roughly ten minutes each time. Jorge discovered that over that time Tanya had written Rubino checks that totaled one hundred thousand dollars, the good portion of her retirement savings.

Checks appeared to have been issued every two weeks, on the same day as one of the phone calls. The last check that was issued by Tanya to Rubino was about one month prior to her death, however, it appeared as if one should have been issued two weeks before her death based on the schedule that had presented itself via the bank statements. Jorge went to speak with Rubino at his office and tried to find out exactly what he was assisting Tanya with that would take so long and cost her such an inordinate amount of money.

"Tanya was involved in a car accident a few years ago. She suffered a broken arm as a result and the person responsible for the accident fled the scene. The police at the time were able to identify him as Julio Sanchez-Giardo, an illegal immigrant who had never been entitled to a driver's license and, of course, had no insurance. Anyway, the police could never find him and Tanya saw my commercial on television and sought my assistance in tracking him down. I employ an excellent private investigator who specializes in things like that, tracking people, and I put him on the case." Rubino leaned back in his chair, pausing for a moment. "We had some good leads, but we just could never put it all together."

"I see. What I don't understand, Mr. Rubino, is why Ms. Moore would spend such a large amount of money to locate someone you both had to know would never be able to repay her?" Jorge waited for his answer calmly. His pudgy face seemed unassuming as he smiled; never tipping off the doubt he had in the legitimacy of Rubino's story.

"Ah, yes, I can see why that would seem strange. All I can say is: you never knew Tanya. She was a pistol, boy. I encouraged her quite often as my expenses started piling up to call it off, that it wasn't worth it. But she wanted justice. It ate her up to know that this guy could do this to her and never pay a cent of restitution." He smiled smugly in return as he looked at Jorge. "Anyway, we worked out a payment plan of sorts. Every two weeks she would issue me a check for my expenses and if she ever desired to discontinue my service she would simply have to give two weeks' notice."

"I see," said Jorge nodding in agreement. "So, what prompted her to end her quest? After almost one hundred thousand dollars worth of investing into it she just suddenly gave it up?"

"Apparently she had gone through nearly all of her savings trying to apprehend Giardo. She examined her finances and decided it was simply too costly for her to continue. I'll never forget the day she let me know she was calling it off. She was very upset about it, as was I. I really wished I could have helped her. But now, detective, I am a busy man as I am sure you are. I know about Tonya's passing and it deeply pains me. I cared for her very much. Even after she stopped utilizing my services I continued to call and check on her. But I'm afraid I can't shed much light on who may have killed her. I don't mean to sound crass, but I really must get back to work, I have a client I must meet with soon."

Jorge simply thanked him for his time and was able to obtain a list of all of his clients over the past two years and began interviewing each of them. Most seemed legitimate.

However, Jorge discovered a pattern of cases Rubino had handled or was handling that deviated from his normal routine. The majority of cases in which he dealt with elderly people seemed to drag on and on for long periods of time and never reached any type of settlement or conclusion. However, each elderly client was charged almost double the rate the rest of Rubino's clients were being charged. Jorge counted eight cases in all over that span where Rubino had pocketed over one million dollars total from his elderly clients without getting them a dime. Six of these cases were still open and pending. The two that Rubino had indicated were closed were Tanya Moore's and the case of a woman named Elsa McMillian. Rubino did not give any indication as to why this case was closed nor would he speak about it, and so Jorge set out to interview her.

When Jorge learned from a neighbor that Elsa had also been murdered, he set his sights on Rubino for not one, but possibly two murders. He contacted the detectives investigating Elsa McMillian's murder and they shared notes. They soon discovered that the cases were identical down to every last detail. The detectives tried to piece a case together against their prime suspect at the time, Pete Rubino.

Like Tanya, Elsa's payments to Rubino had stopped just prior to her death, yet phone calls from him had continued. The theory they formed was simple. Based on the fact that of the eight clients Jorge had uncovered that fit Rubino's pattern of fraud, the two that had stopped their payments to him were now dead. It certainly was prudent to believe they perhaps threatened to expose him in some way. When they wouldn't waver from that stance over the phone, he paid them a personal visit. It would explain the absence of forced entry. Once inside, when the women failed to back down on their threats of exposure, he did the only thing he could think of to silence them. With this theory in mind they arranged for an interview with Rubino to directly challenge him on the murders. But he never cracked, never wavered from his story, not on the fraud and definitely not on the murders. He gave an alibi of playing softball for his firm's team on both occasions.

Rubino was arrested and charged with several counts of fraud and other similar charges. He was quickly able to post bond and the team of now three detectives scrambled to find evidence linking him to the murders in fear he would abscond. However, what they found was something else. They were able to confirm that, even though the murders were separated by seven months, he was, in fact, playing softball at the times both occurred. The detectives wondered: Had he paid someone else to commit these crimes? His bank records did not indicate any large payments or withdrawals at those times, and that would also discredit their theory that he was allowed into the houses because he was familiar with the victims. It appeared that Pete Rubino, though he was guilty of many things, was not guilty of murder.

They began to dig deeper, looking into recent unsolved homicides. In searching the national database, they discovered that two months before Tanya was murdered another murder had taken place in Miami Gardens. The victim was seventy-three-year-old Mary Sanderson. Everything seemed to match up with the other two. No sign of forced entry, she had been strangled, no sexual assault, no items missing, no visible evidence or witnesses. The group reached out to the detectives handling Mary's case and, after comparing notes, all were convinced there was a serial killer at work in South Florida.

After being made aware of the developments and convinced by people whose opinion he respected and valued, the sheriff of Miami-Dade County went about forming a taskforce and trying to absorb the Broward County case into the other two that had occurred in Miami-Dade. This was no easy task. The Pembroke Pines Police Department was reluctant to turn over Tanya's murder investigation and it became a negotiation, with the Chief of Pembroke Pines finally relenting upon the agreement that his department be well represented in the taskforce.

Sheriff Pete Brown began assembling his team, trying as best he could to keep it quiet at first. The original taskforce was made up of approximately forty people, mainly from the Miami-Dade Police Department, but there were also inclusions from the Broward County Sheriff's Office, the Florida Department of Law Enforcement, the FBI, and of course the Pembroke Pines Police Department. Sheriff Brown knew that if and when word of a serial killer got out the people of his county would look to him to combat this individual. Furthermore, when people learned that this serial killer was attacking the elderly, they would be both furious and terrified.

He needed to act swiftly, if not for the safety of his county, for his political future. And so he chose Lieutenant George Greer to head the unit and get things moving along quickly and efficiently. Though Sheriff Brown and George were not close, Sheriff Brown respected George's reputation and experience; specifically that he had the most investigation experience, both as a detective and supervisor of that rank.

Despite the manpower and resources, the taskforce was very slow to pick up any useful information about the killer. Four more victims would surface after their formation and frustration began to mount. The press caught wind of the taskforce and its purpose shortly after a fourth victim was found and began sensationalizing stories, which created a feeling of hysteria in elderly communities and added to the group's chagrin.

They knew little about the killer for certain, and most things they had gathered about him were only theories based on his victims and the crime scenes. An FBI profiler deduced he was most likely a white male between the ages of thirty-five and forty with above average intelligence. They predicted he was not a sexual deviant, like many other serial killers, based on the lack of evidence of any sexual assault taking place prior to or after his victims were killed. They surmised his crimes were about control, and for some reason he felt the need to exhibit control over these particular women. It was unknown if he actually knew them or if they reminded him of someone he actually knew, possibly his mother. These theories, if true, made him unique. And they made him extremely dangerous. As if he killed for no other reason than to kill. As if that was all the pleasure he needed.

They could find no one person with a link to all the victims and ran down thousands of leads over the past year, most of which they were able to discard, but a few were worked into their theories. They were able to determine that the same type of ligature was used in every murder, and that it was some type of soft fabric item, such as a pair of pantyhose or a similar clothing item.

They also had an elderly man who lived four houses away from one of the victims claim that he saw someone walking away from the house shortly after the murder would have taken place. He gave a description of a white man, approximately six feet and two inches tall, wearing long dark slacks, a leather jacket, and a baseball cap. He told detectives that he could not see much of the man's face except that it looked like he had a mustache. He said he saw the man walk from the area of the house to the end of the street and then make a right turn. The only problem with his story was that he waited a week to report it and he was in the early stages of dementia. The man told investigators he had waited so long because he wasn't sure if it really happened. Unfortunately, the taskforce didn't have much else to go by, so they kept the description as a loose reference.

With the taskforce having only one new murder in over nine months and no new leads, slowly, the manpower diminished until it stood at its current level of twenty-seven. The FBI scaled back its involvement as well, although they remained available when needed. Thoughts that the killer was dead or in prison were prevalent, and it appeared that time was running out on the taskforce itself. The cases would soon take a backseat to the ever growing list of other homicides and violent crimes that needed investigating. But until then, George Greer and the rest of the group would carry on with their task at hand.

"OK, does anyone have anything new from last week that might be useful?" George scanned the group of officers who were busy eating their donuts and drinking their coffee. At this point the group mainly consisted of members of the Miami-Dade police department, although Jorge remained as the lone representative from the Pembroke

Pines Police Department, and a few Broward County Sherriff's Office detectives were still assigned to the taskforce as well. "No, no one has anything? All right then. Tips are still coming in every day so be aware of them and let's get going." A few other pertinent notes and minutes later the brief meeting was adjourned. The weekly briefings were more of a formality now than an informative exchanging of ideas.

"Come on, let's go get breakfast," said one of the detectives as he stood up from the table. Tony Petrulia, a twelve year vet of the Miami-Dade Police Department, was a New York City transplant, born and raised in Queens. He had moved to Miami just before being offered the job with Miami-Dade. Tony was an enormous physical specimen of a man. Not so much in height, as he stood at five feet and nine inches tall, but in muscle mass and overall physique. His specially tailored suit barely fit over his biceps and his necktie struggled to maintain its knot. He wasn't considered to be an overly handsome man; his dark brown eyes seemed beady and his nose curled up like that of a pig. He always had dark tanned skin and his short black hair was slicked back with excessive amounts of hair gel. His muscular build seemed to more than compensate for his lack of facial attractiveness, at least in his mind, as he oozed arrogance out of every pore.

"Are you kidding me? We got a ton of leads to follow up on," said the detective who had sat to Tony's left during the meeting. Detective Tim Micheals looked like a string bean in comparison to Tony. He could be imposing himself, standing at six foot one, one hundred ninety pounds, but compared to Tony's physical size he seemed malnourished.

The taskforce had been split up into groups to maximize the number of leads that could be investigated. Jorge had partnered up with two Broward County Sherriff's Office detectives and they ran down leads in Broward County. Tony and Tim had known each other for years and decided they would pair up. As time went by, Tony grew less interested in the tedious work of investigating tips that had come in and more interested in screwing off. He still had the desire to catch the South Florida Strangler and have the notoriety that came with it, but he genuinely believed the killer was in prison, dead, or had moved from the area, and so he brushed off his duties as best he could. Tim also felt like there was some reason for a methodical killer who had been murdering helpless elderly women so frequently to stop, however, he still believed that hard work and a seemingly unimportant clue or tip would crack the case, and he desperately wanted to be the one to crack it.

"Come on, let's go grab a bite. You know I don't eat fuckin' donuts. I need some protein." Tony said with his thick New York accent.

Tim reluctantly agreed to stop for breakfast and the pair went to a local mom and pop breakfast place near the beach that Tony liked. They sat down at a table that faced the ocean and ordered their breakfast. Tim had picked up a newspaper along the way and began reading it. "Jesus, some sick bastard kidnapped and killed a little girl in Boca. What's the matter with people?" Tim asked as he shook his head.

"Yeah, that's terrible," Tony said, continuing to scan the beach. "Holy shit, look at this here. Look, look, look." He nudged Tim's arm with his fist. "Hi girls," he said and waved even though he was certain a group of three young women, clad in bikinis, walking along the beach could not hear him. He stared until they passed and moved out of sight. "Fuck, can you believe those chicks? Isn't it like nine o'clock in the morning? What the hell are they doing out this early?"

"What is wrong with you, man? I'm talking about a little girl who was murdered and you're staring at eighteen-year-old girls. You're drooling, by the way."

"All right, all right, I said it was terrible, what do you want from me, tears? Besides, it's sick fucks that do shit like that that keep us employed." Just then the waitress bent over in between them and placed their plates of food on the table. Her low cut shirt exposed a large portion of each breast as she leaned forward. As she stood upright again, Tony looked at Tim, raised his eyebrows and smiled.

Tony was thirty six years old but never really wanted to be a day older than twenty one. He was married with two children, a ten year old boy and a seven year old girl. Family life mattered little to Tony. What mattered to him was going out to nightclubs and meeting women. He liked drinking heavily and having no consequences for his actions.

He enjoyed his inclusion in the taskforce for many different reasons. It gave his arrogance and feelings of self-importance justification and he knew others would envy and respect him for it. He overlooked the fact that, had he not been originally assigned the Mary Sanderson homicide investigation, he never would have been chosen to be included. Being in the taskforce also gave him a chance to be away from his supervisor in the detective unit he had been assigned to, who he was certain had it in for him because he wouldn't look the other way when Tony came in late or slept at his desk. It was also a great excuse for why he needed to be out all night. He would tell his wife two or three times a week that he needed to be out doing a stakeout for the taskforce, when in reality he was at bars or nightclubs or another woman's home. And of course he enjoyed the freedom he had being out all day checking tips and leads or screwing off, which was what he had begun doing more often.

Tim held a stack of papers that encompassed a small amount of the various tips that had been received via the telephone tip line. In the early days of the taskforce, when there was a lot of information to check and the killer was striking regularly, each group would be assigned different tasks, and the results of those tasks would be discussed the following day in briefing. If any information was looked at as useful, it would be marked on one of the large dry erase boards; the other information would be filed.

Now the taskforce was left with mainly following up on tips that had been phoned in or going over old information. Each group would take a stack of the tips, which were transcribed on paper, along with any biographical data if a name was passed along by the tipster. If the group felt like the tip could possibly be legitimate and helpful, they would pass that information along to Lieutenant Greer. If he felt it was noteworthy he would call a special meeting to discuss it. If not, the tip was filed. Nothing was thrown away.

"All right, we got this guy who claims he saw Elsa McMillian's killer leave her house and is just now calling it in two years after the fact. We have this woman who said her neighbor told her some things about when the South Florida Strangler will strike next, and we have another guy who said his cousin, well, just looks like a serial killer. And those are just the top three tip sheets. Who do you want to see first?" Tim asked as he and Tony walked out of the restaurant and back to their car.

"The chick who knows when he'll strike next. Maybe she's hot."

CHAPTER 11

Anne walked into the examination room and sat on the table. A medical assistant took her blood pressure and asked her a few questions, then left after the advisement that both Dr. Morris and Dr. Hernandez would be in to see her shortly. She sat with her short legs dangling off the edge of the examination table, holding her purse in her lap. Her hip was extremely sore after the walk from her home to the bus stop, then from the bus stop to the doctor's office. Different thoughts crossed her mind as she waited. What she would prepare for dinner that evening, what Louis was doing on that particular day, and if he would join her for dinner.

She thought about her neighbors, whom she disliked. She had seen them on their porch that morning as she walked to the bus stop. They never really bothered her or said anything to her as she passed, but she knew they were selling drugs or who knows what else, and she would get concerned for Louis's safety. When she saw them she remembered how the neighborhood was when she and her late husband had first moved in. It was friendly, upper middle class, and white. Now criminals overran it. She worried they would attack Louis one day or steal the car. He would be devastated by that. He was such a good boy, she thought, and she didn't like street thugs like that bothering him.

Dr. Morris entered the room. "All right, Anne, how are we feeling today?"

"Not too good. It's getting harder and harder for me to walk."

"Well, I think we are all set to do this procedure. Dr. Hernandez will be in here in a second. He will set everything up for the surgery and post-surgery exams. Everything will be fine." Dr. Morris was in a very good mood this particular morning, which was unusual because he usually preferred to scold Anne for one reason or another. Today, however, he was very comforting and reassuring.

Anne was alone again. The thought of another surgery didn't appeal to her. She knew it would be expensive and worried about how she would pay for it. She worried about not being able to be mobile for a while after the surgery. When she had her hip replaced the first time Louis had just been arrested and was preparing for trial. That surgery had been planned since before his arrest, and though she wanted to, she knew she couldn't put it off.

She knew Louis had been going through a lot mentally and emotionally having been accused of a crime he didn't commit, and so she hadn't wanted to further burden him with looking after and helping her. She was working at the hospital at the time and was able to have co-workers and friends come by and help her out for a few weeks. But now she had no idea who she would turn to. She was hesitant to ask Louis to help her; she knew he had his own life and she didn't want to be an encumbrance. She just could think of no one else to turn to and she knew she would have to enlist his assistance at times, although she dreaded asking him for it.

She also worried about the surgery itself. She was getting older and had a heart condition: What if she didn't wake up? What if this was it for her? She worried about Louis. Who would take care of him if she passed away? Before she could ponder these questions further, Carlos walked in.

"Why, hello there. It is good to see you again. How is everything?" Carlos smiled as he looked at her and spoke.

"Oh, everything is fine, I suppose."

"Dr. Morris tells me we are going to go ahead with the surgery. That's good, it's a good thing. Do you have any questions about it?"

"I'm just curious why this is happening and if it will happen again. When I had the first surgery they said it would last forever. That was only twelve years ago. I don't know how much time I have left, but I really don't want to have to do this again."

Carlos smiled and paused for a second before answering. "Well, the doctor who told you it would last forever was wrong. He should not have said that. What happens is the hip replacement implant is made of both metal and plastic, and over time they both wear down. Think of it like a car tire. The more you drive on it, the quicker it wears down. A woman your age at that time was not expected to be as active as you have been, and so the doctor probably assumed you would have gotten twenty years or more out of it. The implant you are getting now is made from a higher quality metal and plastic. I can guarantee you will not need another." He smiled again. "Now, let me ask you, I know you walk to and from the bus stop almost daily, what about around the house, do you do all the household chores or does your son help you out?"

"I do them. Louis lives in his apartment, he takes care of it and I take care of the house."

"Doesn't he ever come over and do things for you at the house? Like clean up after dinner or lock up at night?"

"No, he rarely comes over for dinner anymore and he is never over after dark. He's a very private person."

"Well, I think we are all set, let's set a date, shall we?"

After a date was agreed upon and more small talk was made, Anne was ready to make the trek back to the bus stop and head home.

"I am so sorry, I cannot give you a ride home today I have other patients to see."

"Oh, that's OK, I was planning on taking the bus anyway."

With that, Anne walked out of the office and Carlos could feel the adrenaline pumping through his veins. He was very excited and anxious. This was it; he had waited six long months for this. Since this alter-ego had taken shape he had never gone this long without gratifying his dark callings. He was addicted to the sense of control he got from it. He liked outsmarting and fooling both his victim and the police, flexing his superior intelligence and watching everyone scramble in his wake. He didn't really enjoy the community being paralyzed with fear that he might attack them so much as he enjoyed the community being paralyzed with fear that he could not be caught or stopped. Yes this was it, today was the day—that old feeling was back.

Carlos hadn't really planned on taking such a long hiatus, it just sort of happened that way. After his last victim he felt so badly about neglecting Julia that he decided to surprise her with a cruise. When they returned he took his requisite break from murder and lived honestly, but after a few months his demons began calling again and he started looking for new victims. He perused the patient files, did neighborhood and background checks, but no one seemed to meet his criteria. Another few months went by and still no one struck him as being "the one."

Then Carlos got word from his mother that his father was very ill and he spent weeks tending to him. He had seen his father, Miguel, just a few months prior but hadn't noticed any symptoms. Carlos was devastated. As hard as Miguel had been on him as a child, Carlos loved his father deeply. He cared for his father daily, until his death only one month after Carlos had been made aware of his illnesses. Carlos took Miguel's death very hard and felt strong feelings of guilt for not diagnosing his own father when he had seen him prior to being on his deathbed. He could have at least eased his pain sooner, made him more comfortable. It was a huge blow to his ego and confidence. Maybe he wasn't the doctor he thought he was. It took months before Carlos regained just a bit of his old swagger.

When he met Anne, he had not yet begun reviewing files again looking for his next victim. Maybe he was being anxious in choosing her, one of his own patients. Maybe he was being lazy. Or maybe she truly had spoken to his subconscious and she stood out for a reason. Maybe fate really was crying out for her to be his next victim. Now he felt like he was ready again.

The rest of the day, while at work, Carlos remained in his office. He had no patients scheduled to be seen, despite what he had told Anne, and so he kept the door closed and went over his game plan, again and again. It was precise, it would work, he was sure of it. He would only make one change from his dry run two evenings ago. He would take the bus to the same location, yet he would turn onto the street before J Street so he could come up J Street from the opposite side. He did not want to pass the drug house twice. The more he thought about his interaction with them during his dry run, the more he feared they would be able to put together what he had done. Even though they couldn't identify who he truly was, perhaps someone would have remembered his car from when he drove Anne home. Perhaps the police would discover it belonged to him and begin to show his picture around the neighborhood. It was just too much of a risk. If he was spotted by them and approached he still felt good about being able to get past them without issue, he just preferred to avoid the interaction if he could help it. He knew this change was a gamble having not checked out the other street completely, but he had a good feeling the evening would play out exactly as he planned.

Carlos returned home from work around five-thirty as he usually did.

Julia had been home all day lounging around the house. She had slept until noon and she was just now showered and dressed nicely.

"Hello, my love," he said as he spotted her on his way down the hall.

Julia looked at him for a second then looked back down at the magazine she was reading.

"Hey," she said back unenthusiastically.

"I am sorry, my dear, I have to be the on-call surgeon tonight so I am going into the office around eight." Carlos had used this excuse before. Julia never questioned it and so he continued to use it, assuming she didn't know he was never on-call with the hospital because he technically was not employed by them. The truth was, Julia didn't care one way or another and never really considered it.

Julia's mind began to race upon hearing the news that she had the entire evening to do as she pleased. It was a Monday, and she was hesitant to go out on the town because she feared it would be a waste of her time. She certainly did not want to sit at home alone, however, so she considered her other options. She stood up and walked into the kitchen, where Carlos stood drinking a bottle of water. Their eyes met. She did not really want to speak with him, she just needed to know his location in the house as she had lost track after he walked in and told her of his upcoming absence. Now she was on the spot, in an awkward situation and she knew he would soon be on his way up the stairs and into the bedroom to change his clothes. "I am really in the mood for pizza tonight, what about you?" She said almost seductively, a far cry from her cold and uninterested greeting to him.

"Sure, I could go for some pizza, where did you want it from?"

"Sal's. Would you mind getting it now if I called it in? Please?" She looked into his eyes and smiled for the first time.

"Of course, my dear," he said and walked back out the door. Julia quickly picked up her cell phone off the kitchen counter and called in an order at Sal's Pizzeria for a cheese and pepperoni pizza, then ran upstairs. She reached the bedroom and opened a drawer on her nightstand. She moved some magazines and books out of the way and pulled out a small key. She shut the drawer and entered her large, walk-in closet. In the back of her closet she had several jewelry boxes, some with small locks. She unlocked one of the jewelry boxes and pulled out a different, smaller cell phone and powered it on. She had three voice mail messages that she checked. Two were from a man she had met while out Friday evening and had given her number to. The other was from a wealthy, older man whom she regularly met up with when he came to town. He would take her out for dinner and drinks and the two would stay in a lavish hotel. He told her he would be in town the following weekend and for her to call him when she got the message.

Julia had developed a system over the years for keeping her extramarital affairs a secret. She had her main cell phone number, which she used regularly and Carlos knew about. She also had a disposable, pay-as-you-go cell phone she had purchased using cash at a local convenience store. Every month she would purchase phone cards to use from different convenience stores, and always with cash.

She didn't really know why she went to such great lengths to keep her affairs a secret from Carlos. She had no love for him, they had no children, and she had signed no prenuptial agreement prior to their marriage, so in the event of a divorce she would get half of everything anyway. She often questioned it aloud to herself when she would have to painstakingly hide any traces of her secret life. He had never given her any reason to think he was a violent man, but she feared something else.

She had grown so accustomed to doing what she wanted when she wanted and not having to work for it. She knew that the money she would get in any divorce settlement would not be enough for her to sustain her current lifestyle, and if she were to marry or date any of the wealthy men she had had affairs with or would meet after a divorce she would never be able to get away with what she got away with now. She had the perfect situation with Carlos, and she did not want to give it up.

She realized, as she pondered her evenings plans, that she had not seen her current boyfriend in almost a week, so she dialed him. She left a message on his voicemail for him to call her and stop over that evening. She instructed him to leave her a voicemail message and that she would be able to check it around eight p.m. She shut off the phone and locked it back up, then went back downstairs.

She had been seeing her boyfriend for a while now, but she wasn't enamored with him, and she used the term boyfriend very loosely. She had been with wealthier guys and more handsome guys, but for some reason she stayed with him. He knew her situation, most of it anyway. He knew she was married and he didn't have a problem sneaking around. He did not know, however, that she was also seeing other men when she wasn't with him or her husband.

Carlos returned home with pizza and the two ate and made small talk as they watched television. After eating his dinner, Carlos began preparing for his big night. He got changed into a pair of dark dress slacks and a light blue long sleeve dress shirt. He put on his designer watch and black Italian leather loafers, kissed Julia goodbye, and walked out the door. The rest of his disguise was in the car already. His dark blue New York Yankees baseball cap sat on top of a black leather jacket in his backseat and his fake mustache was in the glove box, though he did not plan to use it tonight. Latex surgical gloves also were in the glove box, and those he would use. Lastly, his most important tool, a wadded up pair of women's pantyhose sat under his seat.

He drove to the grocery store and boarded the bus. Night was falling and the anticipation was building. He finally reached his destination and stepped into the night. He took a deep breath. This was it.

He instituted the change to his original plan and turned down K Street. He soon discovered that K Street was not much better than J Street in terms of residents, but he managed to get down it without a problem. After two quick left turns he was on J Street heading toward Anne's house. Not a soul was outside as he crept in the shadows, no one except for the drug house's occupants. He couldn't see them as he walked, but he could hear them. They were loud and boisterous. He could hear two different female voices and two male voices, one of which he recognized: the voice of the drug dealer with dreadlocks who had confronted him. He tried to stay concealed in the darkness and was soon standing in front of Anne's house. He saw the car in the driveway, and through the window in the top of the garage he could see a light was on, just as it had been when he did his stakeout. He put on his gloves and rang the doorbell. He could hear some commotion inside and a faint voice asking who was there. Footsteps got louder and he could hear someone press up against the door and look through the peephole. "Dr. Hernandez?" He heard in a quizzical tone.

"Yes, Anne, it is me. I was supposed to give you medication this morning to take pre-op and forgot. I just remembered and it is very important you begin taking this medication right away. May I come in and give you the prescription?" Even Carlos was surprised by how convincing he sounded. He heard a door chain unlatch and a deadbolt turn. The door opened up and there was Anne in a nightgown.

"I'm not decent for company, so you can't stay long," she scolded, though she was touched by his kindness in coming all that way just to give her a prescription. Carlos stepped in and Anne shut the door behind him.

The front entrance opened up into the living room where an old couch and recliner sat in front of a small television. The room was dimly lit, the glow of a light from the kitchen and a small lamp sitting on an end table near the couch the only sources of luminosity.

"Good Lord, why are you wearing a jacket?" she asked, but didn't really wait for an answer. "Let me get my glasses," she said as she turned her back and slowly moved to retrieve her eyeglasses from the end table. She leaned over to pick them up but something stopped her from reaching them. Her mind couldn't process what the problem was quickly enough. She struggled to breathe. Her hands reached up instinctively to her throat where she felt something wrapped around her neck. She was suddenly pulled upward and back. She gasped for air and frantically clutched at her throat. Her eyes grew heavy. She lowered her hands and let them dangle.

It was over. Death had come quickly for Anne, whereas her life since the passing of her husband so many years ago seemed to drag on with no relief in sight. Now her suffering was over.

Carlos slowly lowered Anne's body to the ground. She lay face down on the living room floor as he carefully removed the pantyhose from her neck.

This particular killing was a messy one with Anne being only clad in a worn out night gown and underwear. He had to take care not to step in the bodily fluids that soaked the carpet floor. He noticed the staircase to his left. When he reached the top he saw three doors, all closed. He knew Anne's son could enter the home at any time and this left him extremely vulnerable. He hurriedly opened one of the doors and found a bedroom. He opened the next and saw a modest bathroom. He entered, opened the medicine cabinet, and grabbed one of the little orange pill bottles with Anne's name on it, then hurried back down the stairs.

He peered out the window near the door and saw no one, so he felt it safe to exit the house. The door was left unlocked, as were all his exit points for every murder he had committed. He usually preferred to use a backdoor exit, but he knew Anne's son could possibly see him if he did, so he had no choice but to use the front. He quickly removed his gloves and placed them back in his jacket pocket. He froze as he stood in the darkness in front of Anne's house. It seemed as if the occupants on the porch of the drug house had not seen or heard him leave.

He again felt a small rush of anxiety and fear in going back down a small residential side street that he had not scoped out. He felt vulnerable that he did not have a sense of what the street's occupants were like and was concerned he would be seen and remembered as being out of place. He was, after all, wearing a leather jacket in seventy-five degree heat. He also could be spotted and run down by any of the street thugs from the drug house as he walked away. Luckily, it seemed he was able to avoid detection—at least he felt confident he was—and he made it back to the bus stop.

As he waited for the bus he could finally relax and reflect. He smiled as he relived every second. It was smoother than he had even hoped it would be; and a lot quicker. He remembered his conversation with Anne in his office earlier that day, her voice saying she didn't know how much time she had left. He thought back to himself as he stood there and listened to her and that he knew as she was saying it that her time was more limited than she realized. And that now she had no time left. Her time had expired at his hands. Carlos felt powerful, like a god. He had not had these feelings since before his father had passed away and he now remembered how much he needed them. He would not wait very long to feel this way again once it wore off.

Julia sat on the couch with her disposable cell phone in her hands. She had no voicemail message from her boyfriend. She had tried to call him again but she was once again transferred straight to his voicemail. She became frustrated. Not because she missed him or wanted to see him badly, but because she despised being bored and always wanted to be entertained. She called Vikki but Vikki was working and couldn't talk. Finally, she called back and arranged to meet the man she had met Saturday night who had left her two messages.

Carlos always kept a clean set of clothes in his office that he could change into after he arrived there on evenings like this one. He would change into the clean set of clothes, which were generally dress pants and a long sleeve button down shirt, and dispose of the clothes he had worn to commit the murder. This time he also had a pair of shoes waiting for him at the office as he had planned to also dispose of the shoes and watch he had not only worn while taking Anne's life, but that had been identified by the drug dealer who had confronted him during his stakeout.

After getting changed, Carlos settled into his office for the remainder of the night. He did not like to go home after he had completed his plan; he was afraid he would somehow bring traces of his crime with him. He felt even if he did so at work he would be able to explain it better as it was a medical office and, in this instance, Anne had been a patient there. Another reason he had decided not to go home was because he did not want Julia to discover he was wearing a different set of clothes than what he had left in.

He reclined in his desk chair in the small office and turned the television on. He once again thought back to this most recent victim. He thought about her son. A grown man, close in age to himself, who still relied on his mother for everything. Carlos couldn't imagine it. Miguel would never have allowed Carlos to be so dependent. He would have beaten it out of him. Carlos had never met Anne's son, but he wondered what kind of person he was and how he would cope with losing his mother. From what Dr. Morris had told him, Anne's son showed little or no compassion toward her and was very selfish. Carlos suddenly felt a strange sense of accomplishment that he had never felt after killing one of his victims. He felt that maybe this would be what Anne's son needed to finally grow up. Maybe this would make him a man and force him to take care of himself. Maybe he was actually doing him a favor. He smiled and closed his eyes.

CHAPTER 12

As the morning sun spilled once again across the open pullout couch, Louis tried his best to roll over and turn his back in hopes it would go away. After a couple minutes of trying to go back to sleep, Louis opened his eyes and composed his thoughts. He wasn't sure what he would do with his time today, but he knew he was low on gas and money. He would need a replenishment of his funds from his only source of income, his mother, before venturing out to either a park or a mall or a beach boardwalk. Or perhaps he would just stay in his apartment all day. He really did not feel like dealing with his mother, with her whining about her hip and upcoming surgery. The desire he had to spend time with her just two days before had passed. Maybe he would just stay in and surf the internet, which was what he did the majority of the time he was alone in his apartment.

He got up and went to his kitchenette looking for something to eat. He regularly grocery shopped in his mother's cupboards and had just done so Sunday evening when he was over for dinner. To his dismay he had already eaten the entire box of Pop Tarts that he had taken, which fueled his decision for the days plans. If he had to go in and see his mother in order to curb his hunger, he may as well get some money so he could go somewhere later on.

He struggled down the ladder and out of the garage, lumbering to the back door of the main house, his mood starting to sour. It was a hot morning already and he was sweating. He grabbed the door handle and tried to rip the back door open, but it was locked. He looked quizzically at the door. His mother always unlocked the door in the morning, prepared for the rare occasion he wanted to come in for breakfast. She was always up before he was, so why was the door locked? He banged on it and shouted to her but got no response. He turned around and went back up into his apartment and got his keys.

His anger toward his mother for the extra work she was causing him so early in the morning was now boiling over. His breaths were heavy and deliberate. He grabbed the handle once again, put the key in and turned. He flung the door open and burst into the kitchen. "Ma, where the hell is breakfast?" He shouted as he stood in the kitchen, looking at the empty breakfast table. He got no answer. His fuse was lit. Unbelievable, he thought to himself. How the hell is she so lazy? She'll probably blame that hip, he thought again. He sneered as he walked out of the kitchen and into the living room. He stopped abruptly and gasped. His mother was lying on her stomach on the floor, and her head was turned facing him. Her eyes were open. Louis could see that she was dead. He crouched down beside her not sure what to do, not wanting to believe she was gone. "Mom . . . mom . . . MOM!" He cried. He placed his right hand on her shoulder and shook her. That's when he saw the red ring around her neck. He knew that indentation. He realized what had happened. Someone had taken her life while he had been so close by, sitting at his computer in his apartment. He swept the hair back from her eyes and touched her forehead. Her skin was cold. He was suddenly struck by the sobering feeling that her killer may still be in the house. Fear gripped him and he stood back up and began looking around. His eyes caught the staircase. He was convinced the killer was still upstairs. He went back into the kitchen and grabbed the telephone from the counter then went back outside.

"I need the police. Someone broke into my mother's house and killed her," he told the 9-1-1 operator while trying to catch his breath. "Please hurry. I think he's still in the house." The call wasn't for her as much as it was for him. Fear had overcome him and he could only think about being protected from this monster, this animal who had taken his mother's life and would no doubt take his. He needed to feel safe and did the only thing he could think of to get that assurance, losing track of what the police would bring with them when they came to his rescue—an investigation.

Louis stood outside the backdoor and was kept from going back into the house by the plethora of officers who funneled in and out of it. He was now sweating profusely, alternating from leaning against the car in the driveway, to standing, to lying on the grass. He didn't say much, didn't ask many questions. He just sat there. One of the officers assigned to stay with him finally asked if he would like to open up the garage and sit in the shade.

"NO!" Louis quickly shouted as the officer approached the garage door. "I . . . uh . . . I'm fine, it's fine. I could afford to sweat away a few pounds anyway," he said with a chuckle. That was his standard joke when trying to ease suspicion away from himself for something. With his fears of his own safety eased, he was consumed with fear of something else. That they would somehow work their way into his apartment and discover who he really was.

About an hour had passed since Louis had found his dead mother on the living room floor. Police had arrived in swarms anticipating a killer being found inside the home. The house was now overrun with men in suits and uniformed police officers thoroughly searching the property, as well as crime scene technicians. The property surrounding the house had been taped off with yellow crime scene tape.

Finally, two of the men in suits exited the back door of the house and approached Louis, who sat in the grass of the backyard. The men introduced themselves as detectives and confirmed to Louis what he already knew: that his mother had been murdered.

Louis just nodded and frowned, stating, "Yeah, I know, it's terrible," in a soft, barely audible voice.

The detectives looked at each other, then back at Louis. They told Louis they needed him to accompany them to the station to answer some questions so they could find the person who was responsible. Louis froze. A panic flashed in his eyes. He didn't want to leave his apartment vulnerable to an intrusive search. How could he have anticipated this would happen? He had thought of every possible way to cover his tracks, except for this. He cursed himself for calling the police, for inviting this into his life. But what was he supposed to do? he wondered. Let her lay there to rot? How was he supposed to know her killer wasn't still in the house, waiting to take his life as well? Why did she have to be so weak? Why did she have to let herself succumb to this? She had ruined everything. God damn her, he thought.

"I'd prefer not to go at the moment," he said, looking down. "I'm still very much grieving for my mother."

"Sir, it isn't really a request. It won't take long," one of the detectives responded rather forcefully. Louis stood up and followed the detectives to their car. He thought for certain his days were numbered. He began thinking of options, if he was even ever released from police custody. He thought for certain they would find something. He was no crime scene technician, no computer scientist. No matter how hard he tried to scrub away any evidence his crimes had left behind, he knew if they looked hard enough they would find something.

He considered fleeing; as soon as he got let go he would go back to his apartment, gather his things, and drive. But he had no bank account of his own. All the money he ever had he got in cash from his mother—who always carried inordinate amounts of cash on hand because she didn't trust the banks—but he would have to ransack the house to try to find where she kept it, and that was if the police didn't find it first and confiscate it. He was stuck. How could he have anticipated this would happen? he kept asking himself. It wasn't fair; he had been so careful.

The detectives brought Louis into a small interview room and told him they would be right in. They were both anxious. They knew his demeanor at the crime scene was off. He didn't fit the image of a grieving son and he had been too nervous for their liking. They wanted to let him stew for a few minutes before they set out to methodically break him down. As they waited and rehearsed the questions they wanted answered, one of them got a call on his cell phone. After a short conversation, they rehearsed no more, but remained at their desks, continuing to leave Louis alone in the room.

Back on J Street, the large police presence was making the neighbors curious. A crowd began forming out on the street, and news stations were showing up. Word that the South Florida Strangler had finally struck again was already spreading. In law enforcement circles it had been apparent almost instantly. Jorge and the two other members of his task force group, John Youngers and Kristin Mora, had just arrived at the house themselves. Jorge sized up the scene from entry to exit. It was the typical modus operandi for the South Florida Strangler. No sign of forced entry. No real sign of a struggle, nothing noticeably missing.

First responders to the scene had told Jorge that the son was acting strangely and they strongly suspected he could be involved. Jorge recalled the FBI's profile of the killer being a white male, in his late thirties, who chose women who represented something. They had suggested the women may have reminded the killer of his mother. It did seem to fit.

Jorge moved onto the body. It was typically the way the South Florida Strangler would have laid out his victims, although he never posed them. He just set them down after strangling them from behind. Jorge noticed the usual carpet soaked with urine and feces beside the body and stood up from his squatted position.

"Excuse me," he said to one of the crime scene technicians. "I would like a swatch of this whole area when the body is removed. I would like it checked for DNA and hairs," he explained. "Oh, and also, when you check the body for DNA, could you really focus on the back of the victim's neck and see if you can recover anything from her neck or the back of her hair or head?"

It was something they had tried with previous victims but were never successful with. Being that the killer did not sexually assault his victims, DNA had always been hard to come by. But Jorge knew eventually he would leave some behind. The strangler had to perspire or blow some saliva outward inadvertently while in the process of choking his victim. Eventually, they had to be able to find some in useable quantities. At least he hoped they would.

"Wait a minute," he said as the crime scene technician began to walk away after acknowledging that she would adhere to Jorge's requests. "Does this look like a footprint to you?" He squatted down beside Anne's body and examined an indentation in the saturated rug to the left of her legs. It was indeed a footprint, the outline of which was just visible to indicate the size of the shoe belonging to the person who had made it. The crime scene technician laid a ruler beside the impression and photographed it. She then continued on to other tasks with the advisement that she would email Jorge a copy of the picture as soon as she was able.

Jorge and his partners continued to examine the crime scene and tried to get statements from some of the neighbors, but found them all to be uncooperative. Jorge checked the exterior of the house and property but found nothing that could be considered noteworthy. He stopped in front of the garage, which was closed. He asked the officer who had waited outside with Louis if anyone had been inside.

"No, but the son freaked out when I suggested he sit inside the garage to get out of the sun while he waited."

"What do you mean?" Jorge asked, eyeing the old blue car parked in front of the garage.

"I walked over to it like I was going to open it up and he panicked and said he was fine, so I walked away. It was odd."

"Good thing you didn't open it. It's not covered in our search warrant. Anything you would have seen inside of it could have been tossed in court. We are working on a new search warrant for it now." Jorge turned away from the garage and patted the officer on the shoulder as he left.

Jorge, John, and Kristin headed back to the police station to speak with Louis. John had been the one who had called the detectives and stopped them from interviewing Louis. They had wanted to interview him, and probably would have, even though both knew this was a South Florida Strangler case. But when John called and told them not to speak with Louis, they knew they had to pass up their opportunity at cracking the case and making a name for themselves.

Kristin watched through the two-way mirror as Jorge and John entered the small interrogation room. Louis just looked at them, said nothing, and smiled. He had been waiting for forty-five minutes at this point and his thoughts were consumed by what the officers might have found in his apartment. He fully expected to be arrested for his crimes at any moment, and when Jorge and John came in his heart began beating as fast as it ever had.

Jorge introduced himself and John and asked Louis some very basic questions, such as the last time he had seen his mother and if she was expecting anyone to stop by last night. Louis remained on edge, concerned that at any point they would hit him with the news that they had found something he had inadvertently overlooked, but he answered the questions as calmly as he could. He then walked the detectives through his morning up to the point at which he found his mother dead on the living room floor. The more time that passed the more comfortable Louis became and the more he felt like he had once again caught a lucky break. He tried to mask his relief and excitement at that realization, but he found it very difficult not to joke or smile at times.

Both John and Jorge had taken note of Louis's playful candor and general demeanor. He seemed to show no negative emotion about the passing of his mother. Finally, the easy questions were over.

"Louis, I have to be honest wit ya, you seem not to care that much about your momma being brutally murdered," John said in a deep Georgia accent. His skin was almost leather-like from years of exposure to the southern sun. He was balding, but with small patches of red hair still clustered on his head. He had a thick red mustache he kept neatly trimmed. He was only about five foot six and had a typical Napoleon complex.

Louis looked startled by the detective's statement. "What do you mean? Why would I not care? She was my mother."

"Where were you last night?" Jorge chimed in, leaning back in his chair.

Louis tried to comprehend what was going on here. Did they actually think he had killed his mother? Fear once again gripped him, only this time he was not afraid of being caught for the crimes he actually had committed; he was afraid he would be caught for a crime he had not. "I was home, in my apartment all night, why do you ask?" He began to perspire again.

"Was anyone with you?"

"No, I was alone."

"You're kind of an interesting guy, ain't ya? Ain't married, no kids, live wit your momma all your life, but not to take care of her, you live over her garage. No job, no car. What's your story anyway?" John asked.

Louis looked down. "I don't really know what you're asking me."

"I'm sorry, you didn't always live wit your momma. You lived up in Raiford for a few years, idn't that right? Got arrested for molestin a little girl. Was old momma the only one who could stand to be around you after that?" One thing the other two detectives were able to investigate about Louis was his criminal history, which they provided Jorge and John with when they arrived.

"I . . . I . . . I don't know what you want me to say."

"I'm just wonderin why you don't seem very upset. I mean, if it was me and someone cooked fer me, cleaned fer me, paid my bills, gave me money, and was the only one who could stand the sight of me, I'd be a hell of a lot more upset if she weren't there anymore. But you seemed almost relieved when we came in here. Strikes me as peculiar. Don't that strike you as peculiar, Detective Salazar?"

"We obviously know you had access to the house. Your DNA and fingerprints will be all over it," Jorge said very matter of factly.

"It should be all over in there! My mother lives there, I go in all the time, what would you expect?" Louis said sharply.

"Lived. Your mother lived there," John pointed out.

"You're absolutely right, Louis. Your DNA is expected to be in that house all over the place. I agree with you. But where your DNA shouldn't be found is on the back of your mother's hair. On the back of her neck. Where you would have left it as you were choking the life out of her from behind."

"So you do think I killed her? I didn't kill her. She was my mother . . . I would never hurt her. I loved her. She's the only person I've ever remotely cared about." It finally hit Louis. His mother was gone. She was dead. He was alone, left with nothing. He had no job, no money, no one to take care of him. He always loved his mother, as much as his warped and damaged soul would allow him to love anyone. He began to weep.

"Those crocodile tears ain't gonna cut it, friend," John said angrily. "How bout these women, you gonna cry for them too?" He took out several photographs of the previous South Florida Strangler victims and slid them in front of Louis.

"We have the killer's DNA taken from all these victims. We are running it against yours right now. If it matches, well, it'll be too late I'm afraid," Jorge bluffed. "Death penalty. This is your one shot to get in front of this while you can. While I still have a shot at trying to get the death penalty off the table for you. So tell me, what did your mother do to create such anger in you? You found victims that reminded you of her until finally substitutes weren't good enough. You needed the real thing."

"I didn't kill my mother or any of these women!" Louis shouted through his tears. "I've done bad things in my life," he stopped short. He almost blurted it out, his dark secret. He almost came clean on his own victims. As he got caught up in the moment it seemed rational, if he let them know about all the lives he had actually taken, they would have to believe him about the lives he hadn't. But he felt something stop him, something snap him back to his calculating self. He felt a confidence come over him. "I didn't kill anyone. Are you planning on charging me? Do you have any evidence at this moment that suggests I'm connected to any of these women?"

Jorge was taken aback by this sudden change in attitude. He had raised an eyebrow at Louis's statement of having done bad things, but he assumed he was referring to the molestation charge that landed him in prison over a decade ago. "We will. In the meantime, since you have nothing to hide, how about giving us consent to search your apartment and the car?"

"Not without a warrant."

"Well, we don't have a warrant yet, but I will tell you what we do have," Jorge said, trying to remain calm, though Louis's sudden change in demeanor was frustrating him. He thought he was getting close to a confession, however, now he seemed farther away. "We have the right to collect your shoes. So, if you wouldn't mind, go ahead and take them off and put them in this bag." Jorge opened a large brown paper bag and put it on the table.

"Why do you want my shoes? And where is your warrant to collect them?"

"What size shoe do you wear, Louis?" Jorge asked.

"Ten," he replied.

Jorge took another photograph out of the folder that had contained the pictures of the previous strangler victims. He put it on the table for Louis to view. It was the picture of a shoe impression in the rug the technician had emailed him. The ruler beside the impression indicated that the shoe that made the impression was ten inches long.

"I thought you might," Jorge said with a slight smile. "This shoe impression was made after your mother was murdered. It was made by a size ten shoe. You see the way the print is angled? It's in the position you would expect someone to step as they stepped over the body. It was pressed down hard enough to make an impression. As if someone was lowering something heavy to the ground then trying to maintain their balance as they let go and stepped over top of it. Your shoes are going to be evidence. We are working on the warrant at this very moment, and if you choose not to give them to us voluntarily, which you are certainly in your rights to do, then we will simply keep you here until the warrant is issued. Either way, we are getting those shoes." Jorge intentionally tried to be as smug as possible. He wanted Louis to think they had him. He wanted him to think the only way out was to confess. It didn't work.

Louis just nodded in agreement and untied his sneakers. "Here you go," Louis said pleasantly as he placed them in the bag. "I have no doubt you will find my mother's DNA on the bottom of them. You should. I'm sure that is my footprint in that picture. I openly admitted that I discovered my mother's body this morning and squatted down beside her to check to see if she was alive. As anyone else would in that situation. And for me to get back up, after squatting down, I would imagine would take enough force to leave a print like that." Louis was equally as smug in his retort.

Louis's interrogation continued for hours, but he wouldn't budge. Kristin came in and tried to gain his trust and build a rapport, but it was of no use. Finally there was no choice other than to release Louis and drive him home.

CHAPTER 13

They hadn't had time to do much of an investigation, really. Everything had developed so quickly. In the course of a day and a half a little girl went from enjoying an afternoon at the mall with her mother to lying lifelessly on the bank of a canal. And in that short time a family had been torn apart; people's lives were shattered and changed forever. Detectives had run down the typical leads that go along with cases like this: interviewing neighbors, family, friends, all of which had turned up nothing. The first day of the investigation into the actual murder of Ashley Wooten had come and gone in much the same fashion as the short investigation into her abduction; nothing promising to show.

After another subpar night of sleep, Jim and Dan worked feverishly all morning. The problem was that what they had to work feverishly with was less than promising. They were like two hamsters running in a wheel: they worked hard and fast, grasping at anything they could, but got no useful information.

The media had taken a large interest in Ashley's case and ran stories on it in the papers and on the local news. There had even been some national coverage of it. Ashley had become a media darling; the beautiful, innocent little girl who had been savagely abducted and murdered. People were rallying for the cause, crying out for justice to be done. A press conference was scheduled for later that afternoon in which Sergeant Phillips would speak and give the public some new information on the crime itself and appeal to them yet again for some assistance, trying to tap in to the sense of outrage people felt. Tom and Lisa had been told of it and asked if they would like to join Sergeant Phillips. Tom quickly declined the invitation, which Sergeant Phillips accepted and understood.

The crime scene unit's findings from the interior and exterior of the Wooten home yielded several fingerprints that did not match any of the Wooten family members, however, none registered as "hits" when run through the national fingerprint registry. No other useful information was found as a result of the search, which was another roadblock for the investigation.

While the other detectives were out of the office, Andy Sorrenson quietly looked through the recent tips that had come in and came across one that jumped out at him. To this point, the tips that had come in were about vehicles seen leaving the area, possible sightings of Ashley, and of course the tip that led to the rescue of Heather Martin. This new tip had come from a woman who claimed that she had had an affair with Tom Wooten, saying, "He is not the family man he is being portrayed as." Andy was puzzled by it. Tom had a solid alibi for the time his daughter was taken and murdered; there was no chance he had committed the crime. Also, there hadn't been much mention of Tom or Lisa on any of the news broadcasts he had seen or in the papers he had read, so he found it odd someone would feel he was being portrayed as a family man.

He dialed the phone number the tipster, Angela Dombrowski, had left. Angela answered the phone and reiterated her statement that she had, in fact, had an affair with Tom Wooten two years ago and that she didn't believe he was happy with his family life based on statements he had made to her. Angela told Andy she was available all day and would speak to detectives about her claims whenever they wanted to come by, as she had the day off from the salon where she worked.

Still very confused, but intrigued by this possible lead, Andy called Jim. He knew this tip should be investigated, but he had a difficult time understanding how it would help catch Ashley's murderer. He was actually disgusted that someone would try to smear a man's name while he grieved for his only child. Jim, however, saw it differently. While Jim did not believe Tom was directly involved in the murder of his daughter, he thought there was a good chance Tom knew more than he was letting on about something. It had crossed his mind that this scenario may play out. A jilted lover with a motive for payback, or something to that effect.

Jim lumbered into the office and placed a manila folder on his desk. He had walked right past Andy when he entered, without saying a word, even though he could clearly see Andy lunging forward towards him as if he wanted to tell him something. He stood at his desk, and with his back turned to him he shouted, "Where does she live?" There was no response to his question. "Where does she live? You still there, kid? Hello!"

"Uh . . . yeah . . . she lives in," he fumbled for the paper with Angela's information on it. "She lives in . . . oh, here in Boca, just a few blocks away, actually."

"Terrific," Jim said mockingly. He picked up his notebook and walked to Andy's desk to get the information he needed to interview Angela. Andy passed along the piece of paper with her address on it and handed him another sheet of paper. "What's this?" Jim asked as he looked at it.

"Her criminal history. She's been arrested once before for aggravated stalking eight years ago in South Carolina. She also had a restraining order against her stemming from the same incident. I called the department that made the arrest and they said she wasn't arrested for stalking the guy she was fooling around with, who was apparently married. She was arrested for stalking his wife."

Jim maintained his poker face while reading the sheet of paper and listening to Andy, but inside he was excited. He thought maybe he had something; maybe this woman was involved somehow. His mood lightened. "Thanks, kid," he said as he walked to the door. As he grabbed the knob he stopped. "Are you gonna come or what?"

"Sure, I'll come . . . do I need to—"

"Don't make me regret this," Jim bellowed in tone of annoyance, cutting off Andy mid-sentence. "Just get your ass out of the chair and come on. Dan is interviewing neighbors and Bedard is doing God knows what. You're all that's left."

Andy was excited. He, like everyone else, was more or less intimidated by Jim. But like everyone else, he respected him and considered him to be the best detective in the department. Being the youngest and newest detective in the bureau, Andy had never really worked with

Jim, and had never been involved to this extent in such a high profile case.

"So, do you think it's possible she did it? Out of spite, a scorned lover?" Andy asked as they settled into Jim's car.

"I doubt she did it," Jim said as he drove, not really wanting to make small talk but indulging Andy with a short answer.

"Why is that?" Andy probed.

Jim sighed. "Because the little girl was raped before she was strangled. I would think that would be a difficult thing for this woman to do, although I haven't met her yet, so who knows. When you called I was on my way back from the M.E.'s office getting the autopsy report, so as you can imagine I'm in just a great mood to chit chat." The manila folder Jim had placed on his desk was the medical examiner's report. Ashley's official cause of death was ligature strangulation. The object used to strangle her was most likely something soft like an article of clothing or pillowcase or anything that could be wrapped around her neck that wasn't abrasive enough to pierce the skin as it tightened. She had been sexually assaulted, but they found no DNA from her killer. Her short time partially submerged in the canal was enough to destroy any significant physical evidence her killer may have left behind. They did, however, find several small tan fibers on her body consistent with the material used to make quilts or comforters, which seemed to indicate she was most likely wrapped in some type of blanket and transported to the canal bank post-mortem. The medical examiner placed the time of death sometime around two a.m. Sunday morning.

Andy looked embarrassed even though he had no way of knowing. He was desperate to redeem himself and not appear stupid in front of Jim. "Well, you never know, there have been several documented cases in which a woman will abduct another woman and fake a rape using a foreign object to divert suspi—"

"What the hell happened?" Jim interrupted, looking at Andy instead of the road. "You never said anything before. You were always so quiet. But get you out of the office and you don't shut up. Just use this as a learning experience and let me handle this interview. OK?" Jim turned his attention back to the road and shook his head.

They pulled up in front of the modest, one-story yellow house and met Angela at the front door. The home was built in the Spanish style and appeared to be very old yet well maintained. It was not in one of the numerous gated communities in Boca Raton, but it was in a respectable area never the less.

Angela had been watching for them for over an hour. She was very anxious to tell her story. A short, very slender woman, Angela was very attractive. Her blonde hair was tucked back into a ponytail. Her blue eyes were deep and seductive. Despite it being her day off and her claim that she would just be lounging around the house all day, she appeared to be freshly made up. "Come on in," she said as she held open her front door. Jim and Andy sat at the kitchen table across from Angela as they would in an interrogation room. "I just wanna say, first off, that I feel terrible for that little girl. So awful." She shook her head side to side and pursed her lips together.

"What is your information for us pertaining to this case?" Jim said very bluntly.

"Oh, OK, wanna get right into it. I see." Angela seemed annoyed that Jim wouldn't let her continue to express her feelings of sorrow for Ashley. "Well, uh . . . about two years ago . . . I wanna say two years ago, but it might have been closer to two and a half," she raised her eyes to the ceiling as if it were helping her remember. "Anyway, we'll say two years ago, my computer busted and I remembered seeing this little computer repair place in the plaza where I get my nails done, so I stopped by one day. I talked to this really nerdy guy, what was his name?" She asked herself, again raising her eyes to the ceiling.

"I know who you're talking about, his name isn't really important," Jim said, as calm as he could sound in his increasingly aggravated state.

"OK, I guess it doesn't matter," Angela said looking at Jim, again seeming annoyed that Jim wasn't allowing her to tell the story the way she wanted to. "Anyway, he tells me that I can either bring it in and they can fix it there, or I can have the boss come to my home and fix it at my convenience. And just then, it was weird, Tom comes walking out, you know he's the boss and all, and says hello and introduces himself. He seemed really nice, like a nice guy, and so I ask if he can come by that night to fix the computer and he tells me he can. So he comes by and works on the computer and we are making small talk the whole time. I just felt like he was a really nice guy, and you know, he's good looking too, and, you know, I was drinking some wine and I guess one thing just led to another." With that Angela abruptly stopped.

"What exactly does that mean, one thing led to another? You need to be more specific."

"We fucked, is that specific enough for you? Need to hear me say it? I'm not proud of it, you know. I don't regularly screw married men. It just happened." Angela's eyes no longer seemed seductive; they now reflected anger, fear, annoyance, insanity.

Jim knew she did not kill Ashley herself. Killing a child would take a certain type of individual, and in Jim's experience, generally those individuals weren't women. He knew there were very highly publicized cases of mothers killing their children, but there were very few cases of women abducting and killing unrelated children. What he was trying to figure out was if she had hired someone else to do it or if everything she was telling them, though it may have been true, was a waste of their time as far as Ashley's murder was concerned.

"All right, I understand, so continue with your story."

"So anyway, we saw each other a few times after that. He would always tell me he was unhappy at home and he didn't like being tied down, stuff like that. I'm not saying he did it, but I'm just saying it wouldn't surprise me."

"So how did the relationship end?" Jim asked, ignoring her insinuation.

"It just . . . ended. I knew he was married, and he wasn't going to leave his wife even though he was miserable with her. He used to tell me that all the time, that he hated going home at night."

"It just ended? Just like that?" Jim prodded.

"Yeah . . . yup," she said as she looked down at the table.

"Come on, I have a hard time believing that. I know you don't like letting men walk away from you without some type of punishment." Jim knew what was coming. He knew from the minute that he saw Angela that this interview would end badly. He looked her square in the eyes and awaited her response.

"What the hell is that supposed to mean?" She snarled, returning his glance with eyes that burned. She seemed to be on the verge of leaping over the table and attacking him.

"Where were you this past weekend? Saturday, specifically?" Jim tried not to smirk as he asked.

"You think I did this?" she shouted. "Oh, you are sick." She tilted her head back as she made this statement, as if her body was slowly recoiling in disgust from the top down.

"I know you have a history of bothering family members of men that aren't interested in you anymore."

"Get out! I want you out of my house!" Angela stood up and pointed at the door. "I try to help you people and this is how you treat me? Like a suspect? I'll sue your asses."

On that note Jim and Andy exited the residence in the fashion Jim had envisioned they would.

"So what now?" Andy asked as the two got back in the car.

"Now we go see Tom Wooten."

Andy was a little surprised by this, wondering what there would be to gain by confronting a man who had just lost his daughter with these seemingly unimportant allegations. But, he knew if Jim thought it was a good idea then there must be some merit in it, and so he decided just to sit back and observe.

Jim pulled up in front of the Wooten home and shifted into park. Media outlets that had crowded the street and sidewalks surrounding the home just the day before had dissipated a little, but some remained. Andy reached for the car door handle, but Jim stopped him.

"Listen good. This is not going to be an interrogation. This is giving him a chance to come clean about mistakes he has made in his life that may help us catch his daughter's killer. We aren't going to push this, not today. Keep. Your mouth. Shut." Jim let go of his grip on Andy's left wrist and the two exited the car amid questions from various reporters and the sounds of a few camera shutters. They were greeted at the door by Lisa's father, who shook Jim's hand and invited them both in. Many family members, most of whom Jim did not know, gathered around them waiting for some kind of news, which was why they assumed Jim and Andy had come. Tom was among them, but Lisa was not. "Uh, I'm sorry to intrude folks, but I just need to speak with Tom for a moment, privately, if you don't mind." Mark looked at Tom as if to inquire if it was all right and if he was feeling up to it.

"Yeah, sure, let's uh . . . go on the back deck." Tom said sounding exhausted, and led Jim and Andy outside to the deck area, shutting the sliding glass door behind them. "What's going on?" he asked as he placed both hands in his pants pockets.

"Tom, listen, I know you're going through a lot right now, and I apologize, but you need to come clean with us before I can do my job and find who did this. I think you know what I'm talking about." Jim saw the look of fear in Tom's eyes. He saw his nervousness and guilt. "We spoke with Angela today."

Tom rubbed his forehead roughly with his right hand. What little color had been there rapidly disappeared from his face.

"We are not here to judge you, or rat you out, but we have to know, is there anyone else that may have reason to be upset with you? And it doesn't just have to be from an affair. For any reason."

Tom folded his arms at his chest and looked at the wooden slats of the deck. It was only three days ago his little girl had stood where he stood, then had run around in the yard just beyond it. He took a deep breath. "All right, I'm not perfect. I'm not even a good guy, I guess. I love my family, I do . . . I did. I just wasn't very strong. Angela was one of the biggest mistakes of my life. She was beautiful and she was sexy and she was . . . absolutely insane. She would show up almost daily at work and I would have to scramble to explain to Rick and Kurt why she was there. Finally, I ended it, or tried to. She threw two kitchen plates and a glass at me as I ran for the door. She would call my cell phone, she would wait for me in the parking lot. I didn't know what to do. I had to try my best to keep Lisa from finding out, which was hard. She isn't stupid. One time she must have been watching the shop from the parking lot and she saw Lisa and Ashley come visit me, so she came inside. I was terrified. And that's exactly what she wanted. She just made up some bullshit story about needing someone to come to her house and fix her computer, which thankfully Rick and Kurt didn't call her out on because I'm sure they remembered she had been in there for the same thing not too long before. She even talked to Ashley," Tom swallowed his tears as best he could, "telling her what a great dad she had." His voice cracked and softened to a breathy tone. "Then one day, about six months ago, maybe ten, she just stopped. I figured she found someone else and finally decided to leave me alone. But maybe she was planning something." He paused then started again, "If she did this, I don't think I can live with myself. My daughter was innocent, why not punish me directly?" For the first time he looked up at Jim, as if waiting for Jim to give him an answer.

"All right, we need to know of anyone else. Here's a notepad and pen, write down names and addresses if you remember them. And if you have had other affairs, even if things ended amicably, still write the names down. We still need to speak with them." Tom nodded and began writing.

The work day was quickly drawing to a close and everyone was finally back at the station. Dan's interviews had yielded no productive information, though he still described each of them to Jim. Jim relayed the details of the medical examiner's report, as well as his interviews with Angela and Tom. He then tossed the notebook Tom had written in on Dan's desk.

"Wow, I guess you were right. He was hiding something. So is it likely this Angela was involved?"

"I don't know," Jim said leaning back in his chair. "She is crazy . . . I mean like certifiably nuts. But to go this far, I don't know. I mean, I guess it's possibly she found some pedophile willing to do all this for money, but it just seems so unlikely. I just don't know. I'm leaning away from her, but as of now, she's the only suspect we have."

"That may not be necessarily true," said Paul Bedard as he walked into Jim and Dan's desks. "On the mall security video there is a guy, big fat guy, who bumps into and knocks Ashley to the ground. It looks like he apologizes and exchanges pleasantries with both Ashley and her mother before they leave and he sits on a bench. That in itself might be nothing because it looked like Ashley was actually more at fault than he was. But I kept looking in the other video frames for this guy, and sure enough, he shows up in quite a few. He's never too close, but he always seems to be lingering behind. He leaves about twenty minutes before they do, but out of the same exit. Unfortunately there is no video of him getting into a car, so we lose him there, but there is something else."

"What is it, Bedard?" Jim said rolling his eyes.

"I was able to zoom in the best I could to get a somewhat clear image of his face. Still kind of blurry but it's visible. I compared him to the stack of Palm Beach County sex offenders I had and he didn't appear to match any. But then I tried to compare him to some Broward County sex offenders and he seems to fit the physical description of this guy, Louis Bradford." Paul handed Jim a printout of Louis Bradford's sex offender registry, which had his picture, height, weight, address, and a description of what crime he had committed to be deemed a sex offender. "He lives in Davie. I thought we could speak with Lisa Wooten tomorrow and see if she remembers him and if she saw him again, maybe in the parking lot area or outside of the mall, then head down to Davie to interview him."

"We? We, Bedard? What is this 'we' shit?" Jim asked as he looked at the printout.

"Come on, I found this one, at least include me in the interview."

"Since I'm feeling nice today," Jim looked up abruptly at Dan and interrupted himself, "I took the kid with me today, by the way."

"Oh yeah? How'd he do?" Dan asked. Jim just shook his head in response.

"Since I'm feeling nice today, taking the kid out and all, I'll let you tag along on our trip to Davie. But you are not speaking with Lisa Wooten. The woman has been through enough, she doesn't need to be paraded in front of a million different detectives. Especially ones who seem giddy about their part of the investigation into her daughter's murder." Jim paused for a minute and looked hard at the sex offender registry flyer Paul had given him.

"Bradford . . . that name sounds familiar. He ever been arrested up here before?" Jim asked in a more cordial tone than he had initially started with.

"Nope, only arrest was for the sex offense in Davie."

"Huh, I feel like I've heard that name before." Jim said as he strained to search the recesses of his memory bank.

Night was falling on the Wooten home, and family and friends were leaving. It had been the hardest few days of all of their lives, from cousins to friends, and, of course, for Tom and Lisa. The burden of making funeral arrangements fell to Tom, with assistance from Mark and some other family members. Lisa had been inconsolable since learning her daughter had been murdered. After being called by Tom, the dentist from the office she worked at came over and provided her with a prescription for oxycodone, which Tom filled and had given her. No other family members knew of this, except for Mark, and Tom had just told the others she had taken a few sleeping pills. She had, in fact, taken a sleeping pill as well as the oxycodone and the combination had pretty much knocked her out for the entire day, allowing her to get some rest for the first time since Friday evening.

After the initial pain and chaos had washed over her, she began feeling something just as strong as grief. Guilt. Though she had just started to question herself and what she could have done differently before she was put in her current, almost coma like state, the guilt was the most intense feeling she had ever experienced. The combination of grief and guilt made it almost impossible for her to think, eat, or sleep on her own.

Tom felt his own guilt as well though it wasn't as consuming as Lisa's. He worried that he may have been responsible for Ashley's disappearance. What if he had just told the detectives right away about Angela? Could Ashley have been saved? He had hoped his infidelities could continue to be a secret, despite the intrusive police investigation. When he had learned of his daughter's disappearance he thought there was a chance one of his mistresses could have been involved, Angela specifically, but he made the decision to remain quiet about their existence. Now he dealt with another emotion that Lisa had yet to contend with. Shame. He knew eventually everything would come to light and be out in the open. His philandering, his withholding information from the police, everything. He knew Lisa couldn't take that kind of admission from him right now. She was barely hanging on. He knew he should tell her, at least about Angela, but it would have to wait for now.

The house was almost empty. Only Mark remained, and he was already asleep on the living room couch, his makeshift bedroom. Tom sat alone at the dining room table, the same table he had sat at only two days before, watching Ashley chase the dog and run in the yard. As hard as he tried to suppress them, memories of Ashley flooded his thoughts. He remembered when she was born and how he wasn't sure if he was ready to be a father, or if he would even be a good one. But then he held her for the first time and all his doubts slipped away.

He remembered the trips they had all taken. Seeing her happy and excited was the most enjoyable thing he had ever done. And he remembered that last hug he had gotten from her, as she ran to him from across the living room right before he left Saturday morning. He wished he had squeezed her tighter. He wished he had lingered just a little bit longer. He wished he had never left.

As the tears trickled down his cheeks he also thought of the future and how nothing would ever be the same. No trips to plan with her in mind. No more hugs. Nothing would ever be as enjoyable. He realized his life was now going to be separated into two categories: a before and an after, at least that's how he would forever view it. No matter what occurred from now until his own death, he would forever view his memories as before and after the death of his daughter, as if a line had been drawn in his life. He knew others would only see the after; nothing he had ever done before would matter. They would see him and immediately think of a tragic incident, nothing more. He would never get over her death and knew he could never escape it. It was who he was now. A tragic figure.

CHAPTER 14

As morning coaxed him out of his slumber, Louis opened his eyes and gradually pulled himself out of bed. He struggled to focus and gain his bearings as he stumbled through the small apartment and into the bathroom. The apartment was just as he had left it before being hauled into an interrogation room the day before. He was certain the police would have searched it while he was away and found some type of evidence of his crimes, but when he returned he was relieved to find out that wasn't the case. Nothing was displaced, nothing was missing that he was aware of. However, as he brushed his teeth and looked at himself in the small, dingy mirror he knew his time was running out. He knew that his luck was bound to change, and probably sooner rather than later now that he was an official police suspect.

He was a suspect in the murder of his mother, and the murders of the seven other women that comprised the South Florida Strangler's death toll. Though he was a serial killer himself, he never thought of himself as such. He had taken the lives of eight little girls, but he saw the murders as collateral damage of sorts. He hadn't wanted to kill any of them. He derived no enjoyment out of it. He found it to be a necessary evil; he couldn't simply release the girls after what he had done, and he saw it as his only option. He felt he had nothing in common with a man that simply wanted to murder.

He knew there would be no evidence linking him to the South Florida Strangler cases, but he also knew that as the police tried to dig some up they would eventually uncover other evidence to the crimes he had committed. He was at a crossroads. He knew he had to flee. Still, he felt conflicted about leaving the only sanctuary he had ever known. About leaving his mother. As long as he remained in that apartment and on that property he could hang on to her. He would still be able to feel her presence.

Louis made his way down the ladder and through the garage. He opened the door and stood facing the street. The glare from the sun temporarily blinded him. He felt its warmth on his skin. The morning air filled his nostrils. He only heard a soft breeze blowing. He closed his eyes for a moment, then opened them again. As his sight came back into focus he saw a yellow streamer flapping in the breeze at the corner of the property near the sidewalk. As the streamer flapped he could read in black bold print the words DO NOT CRO on it. Suddenly, the surreal moment he was having with Mother Nature was gone, he was once again reminded of the predicament he was in, and he closed the garage door and made his way to the house.

Police had still been there when he returned last night, still searching his mother's house. He paid them no attention and hid away in his apartment. He wasn't sure what time they had left or if they would be back.

He let himself into the kitchen and almost instinctively looked at the breakfast table. It was empty, as it had been the day before when he glanced at it. His mind flashed back to a time when it was full of foods he loved, specially made just for him. It wasn't so long ago, just three days in fact, that he had enjoyed dinner at that table with his mother. Though he had complained about the food as he often did, he still enjoyed it. He still remembered the smell of her meat sauce as clearly as if it were simmering on the stove at that moment. He could see her there, cooking for him. He felt like she had just been there, with him in this place, only moments before, but he knew she was gone now, never to be there again. He glanced toward the living room, the place of his gruesome discovery, and the nostalgic images faded from his mind.

He walked a little farther and stopped. His mother no longer lay on the floor as she had when he found her. Large portions of the carpeting had been cut and removed. The room was dark, at least darker than it usually was at this time of the morning. Louis looked around the room as if drinking it all in one last time. He looked down at his mother's final resting place. Despite the irony, he could not put together his mother's demise with the lives he had taken. He wasn't a killer, he had always told himself that, and thus he never felt remorse for killing. But this, to kill an elderly woman for no reason, was incomprehensible to him.

Up to this point, he had kept his mother's murder separated from his feelings. Emotions had overtaken him at one point while being interrogated by the police, however, he quickly was able to suppress them in order to save his own skin and focus on evading any admissions of guilt. But since that point it was as if his brain knew his mother was dead, but it kept that information from the emotions that should have come with that knowledge. Until now.

As he looked at the place his mother had been savagely attacked and laid for him to discover, the tears began to flow. He felt alone. He once again longed for her companionship. She had supported him, both financially and emotionally. As much as he had always tried to rationalize the monster he had become, he knew in that moment that he was one, and that she probably knew it all along. But she had loved him and supported him anyway. She had never expected anything from him; she let him do what he wanted and be who he wanted. And this was who he had wanted to be. A stalker. A pedophile. A killer.

As the emotions came, he now understood there was no distinction between the lives he took and the lives his mother's killer had taken. He finally felt what his victims' families felt. Shame overwhelmed him for the first time. He felt guilt. He felt remorse.

As he stood examining the room, he noticed motion outside the house through the sheer curtains of the front window. He moved closer to it, stepping over the place where his mother had laid as if she was still there. He pulled back the curtain and observed a dark blue sedan with dark tinted windows parked on the street across from the driveway. The car was running and there was a spot on the pavement next to the driver's side front door as if someone had dumped something out the window. He knew it was the police, and he knew he was being watched.

As it turned out, Louis was correct, it was a police officer in the car and that police officer's job was to, in fact, watch him so he didn't flee. The South Florida Strangler taskforce was in pursuit of Louis, working as hard as they could to somehow at least link him to his mother's slaying. The taskforce had a briefing earlier that morning where Jorge told them of the recent developments, including the announcement of a suspect, Louis Bradford. Despite the promising new leads, Lieutenant Greer did not pull every available unit off of their current assignments to assist Jorge, John, and Kristin. Instead, he maintained that the Broward County trio should conduct this investigation and if they needed assistance it would be provided to them at that time. Feeling that time was of the essence, the trio did not physically attend the morning briefing in Miami, instead they relayed their information via teleconference from their headquarters in Broward County.

Not all things were looking up, however. A devastating blow had already been delivered to the investigation. While Jorge and Kristin briefed the task force of the most recent killing via teleconference, John had written and delivered a search warrant request for Louis's apartment and the car he shared with his mother. But to the group's surprise and disgust, the search warrant had not been granted, at least not in its entirety.

The judge did allow for a search of the garage itself, however, he would not allow for a search of the apartment above it, or the vehicle. He had reasoned that the apartment, despite its close proximity to the home in which the killing took place, should be deemed a separate residence even though there was no lease agreement. He further stated that no evidence existed to search this separate residence for any evidence of the crime of murder thus far.

He deemed that the vehicle, due to the fact that the registration was in both Louis and Anne's name, belonged to both of them equally and both needed to give consent. Since Anne was no longer capable of giving it, the vehicle was now the sole possession of Louis and his consent would be needed to search. He also again stated that no evidence was presented to suggest the vehicle or its owner were involved in the crime of murder. Nor had Anne even driven the car within a reasonable amount of time before her death that evidence could be obtained from it.

Lastly, the lone victory for the team, the judge did allow for a search of the garage to be completed only on the bottom floor based on the fact that it should be considered part of the main house, even though it was not attached, and that it consisted of "common area" and not a residence. Initially there had been some confusion on if Louis's apartment encompassed the entire garage or just an upstairs portion, which was the reason it was not included in the original search warrant of the main house. However, if they wanted to get in to the apartment and car, the group would have to come up with some type of hard evidence suggesting Louis was involved in this or any other crime before they would be allowed to search them.

To further add pressure to the team, the Sherriff's Office had allowed for an officer to be taken off the road to tail Louis Bradford and ensure his whereabouts were known at all times. However, this was an extremely temporary thing, and would only be allowed for, at most, a few more days.

The team headed over, along with some crime scene techs, to the Bradford home armed with the search warrant for the garage. They located Louis, who was still in the main house and served him with the warrant, which he just glanced at and didn't say a word in response to, though the detectives didn't give him much of a chance to respond before they made their way to the garage. They entered the musky-smelling, cluttered area and got to work, meticulously searching for anything that might help build their case. After about an hour, it seemed that every inch of cement was thoroughly inspected, but the smoking gun they hoped for was nowhere to be found. The garbage cans were empty and an inspection of the floor and walls yielded no evidence of a violent struggle ever taking place there. The only minor victory for the team was the discovery and collection of several small hairs, but they would have to be analyzed and matched to a Strangler victim to be of any help.

Jorge stopped and took a deep breath as he stared at the door cut into the ceiling and the string dangling from it that stopped just above his head. It was so close he could reach out and grab it and with one good pull the door would open, leading to what was certain to be a treasure trove of evidence above. But he couldn't, and that evidence would have to remain hidden, at least for now. Jorge could feel frustration building, which was very uncharacteristic of him. This was the biggest case of his career and he felt very strongly that Louis was his guy. He had to be, they had never been so close on a suspect before. Even though the physical evidence was not there, and he had yet to link Louis to the other victims, he felt the circumstantial evidence screamed out that Louis was it. The team wrapped up their search with the hairs and little else and left.

In an attempt to relieve his frustration, perhaps get back to the investigator he had been prior to the South Florida Strangler taskforce and the obsession he had begun to feel with his role in it, Jorge decided to look at this homicide as an individual case. He had a suspect, but no evidence to support it yet. He needed to follow up on other possible leads. He started with the partial timeline that had been created of the events of Anne's final day. A calendar had hung on the kitchen wall on which Anne had written appointments and obligations. For that day, Monday, Anne had written only one thing, "Dr. Morris 1 PM." Jorge was able to get the address to Dr. Morris's office from one of the pill bottles retrieved from the upstairs bathroom medicine cabinet and headed there to speak with him.

Dr. Morris had heard on the news of Anne's death and was still upset about it when Jorge spoke with him. He had a personal connection with a lot of his patients, but he felt strongly about Anne because she had been with him as a patient for so long. More importantly, though he was hard on her at times, he had always felt sorry for her. He knew she had had a hard life with her husband's death and raising a son on her own. Then, of course, dealing with the son she had raised. Dr. Morris explained to Jorge that he had only spoken with Anne for a moment at the beginning of her appointment and then he turned her over to his associate, Dr. Hernandez, who was to perform her hip replacement surgery. Dr. Morris was then asked about Anne's son, which he was quick to respond to.

"Did he do this?" Dr. Morris fired back gruffly.

"We don't know yet, do you think he is capable of doing it? Had she ever said she was afraid of him before?"

"No, she never seemed afraid of him. He always seemed like kind of a pussy to me . . . pardon my language, I just never cared for him."

"Why is that?"

"He treated her like garbage, and she supported him no matter what. He used to make her take the bus here so he could have the car. And he never worked, so who knows what he needed the car for that was so damn important. The few times he did pick her up he would act pissed off that he had to do it. He never looked me in the eyes. He just seemed like he would melt if he was talked to sternly or put in his place. But Anne would never do that. She babied him all his life."

Jorge wrapped up his conversation with Dr. Morris and moved on to Dr. Hernandez, who was in his office. "Please, call me Carlos," he said as the men shook hands.

"All right, Carlos, you met with Anne Bradford yesterday at 1 PM, is that correct?"

"Yes, I heard about what happened. Terrible. She was a wonderful woman. They said the man who killed her was that serial killer, is that true?"

Jorge remained straight faced and gave a noncommittal response of, "We aren't sure yet." He quickly followed with, "Did she seem afraid or did any of her actions seem odd at all during your appointment?"

"No, she seemed anxious to have her hip replaced. It had begun to really bother her."

"Did she mention any plans she may have had for the remainder of the day?"

"No, she took the bus home, but that was normal."

"Did she ever mention her son to you?"

Carlos paused for a moment. He knew what this question meant. It seemed perfect, he thought. Her son would be the perfect suspect. "She mentioned him a few times, yes."

"Did she ever express to you any fear of him?"

"No, she just seemed worn down by him. My understanding was he was angry with her all the time."

"Did she say why he was always angry with her?"

"Not specifically, it just seemed anything she asked him to do he would get upset about. It seemed she was invading on his lifestyle too much."

"All right, and about what time did she leave here? Do you recall?"

Carlos looked up toward the ceiling. "Well, usually appointments last around a half hour, and we did schedule her hip replacement surgery as well, so she was probably here in the room for about thirty-five minutes, but I'm not sure what time it was exactly when she was brought in. Occasionally appointments do not start on time," he smiled sheepishly with this admission.

"OK, Doctor, thank you for your time." Jorge shook Carlos's hand again and the two men locked eyes. Jorge paused and gazed quizzically into Carlos's eyes.

Carlos smiled back at him, but he could tell something wasn't right. Something was going on in the detective's head.

"You know something," Jorge said finally, breaking the silence. "I know who you are."

Carlos was confused by this. Was this some sort of trick? Had this detective known along it was him and had been toying with him up to this point? Did this detective recall his involvement in the Rebecca Sullivan case? Had he made a large mistake striking so close to home once again? For the first time since his initial murder, he was afraid. Afraid he had made a mistake. Afraid he had been caught.

"Years ago," the awkward pause was finally broken, "I worked a taskforce, it was a gambling ring. Anyway, I worked with a guy from Boca Raton, Jim Brekenridge. He told me his mother had just had shoulder surgery and I'm fairly certain you were the doctor he said performed it. Carlos Hernandez at Ft. Lauderdale Hospital. I think I wrote it down because my mother was having similar problems with her shoulder at the time."

Carlos breathed a sigh of relief. "Yes, yes I did. Her first name escapes me at this moment, but I do remember him, the police officer. He was a very large man."

"Yes, Jim is enormous. Anyway, he said you were excellent and highly recommended you. Said you treated his mother very well. Weird, huh? I never forget a name though, which is always a good thing in police work." Jorge smiled.

"Yes, it certainly is a small world. How is she doing anyway?"

"I haven't talked to Jim since that particular case closed, so I don't know. Again, thanks for your time, Doctor, I have to be going." With that, Jorge left the office having obtained an image of Louis as an uncaring, angry son. He continued to fit the profile.

CHAPTER 15

Jim and Dan pulled up in front of the Wooten residence and slowly walked to the front door. Jim had spoken to Tom prior to their arrival and told him they needed to show Lisa a picture and speak with her. Tom had agreed, but seemed apprehensive, stating she was still taking anti-anxiety medications as well as sleeping pills and at times was unable to focus. The truth was she was actually taking oxycodone without a legitimate prescription for it, but Tom decided he should leave that part out when speaking with police. He met the detectives at the front door and led them into the living room where Lisa sat on the couch.

Lisa's appearance had become almost unrecognizable from when the detectives first met her on Saturday. Her hair was tangled and looked like it had gone unbrushed since the moment she realized her daughter was missing. Her once flawless skin now was red in spots and small areas of acne showed through without makeup to disguise them. Purple bags were prominent under her eyes. She clutched a mug of coffee and mustered a "hello" as Jim and Dan stood in front of her. Jim apologized for bothering her and told her they had been reviewing the security tapes from the mall on the day Ashley was abducted. He showed her the picture of Louis Bradford and asked if she recalled seeing him at the mall. It was the photo from his sex offender registry, however, all the information around his photo, including that he was a sex offender, had been cut out. Jim did not want the information to influence Lisa's memory in any way. She clutched the picture in her hands trying hard to focus on his face.

"I don't recall seeing him, no." Lisa said, squinting and still trying to focus on his face.

"At one point Ashley bumped into him and she fell to the ground, do you remember that?" Dan said in a soft, calm voice.

"Yes, I do remember that." She took a closer look at the picture. "Yeah, this is the guy she bumped into, but that was her fault, she wasn't paying attention. Right?" She trailed off and seemed confused, looking up at Jim as if she was expecting him to complete her memory.

"That did appear to be the case, yes. He was also seen later on to be leaving around the same time as you. Do you remember seeing him again any other time on your trip, maybe in the parking lot or in your neighborhood? Had you ever seen him before?" Jim asked as personably as he could, yet he still came off as very rushed. He was anxious to speak with what he felt was his first real suspect.

Lisa's eyelids opened and closed very slowly. She said nothing, just shook her head no. Guilt had already overcome her. Guilt and sorrow. She felt very strongly by now that this was her fault. Her inattentiveness. Her lack of supervision. Her selfishness. It had all led to her daughter being kidnapped and ultimately murdered.

Tom also felt that way. In all, he had written the names of five women on Jim's pad. And those were only the ones who lived locally. When Lisa stopped accompanying him on his out of town trips he became more active in the nightlife while away. And, of course, interactions during in-home repair calls like the one he had had with Angela were common as well.

"Do you think this man is responsible for kidnapping my daughter?" Tom asked, finally breaking the silence, reaching for the picture. Of course what he really meant was, was he responsible for killing my daughter, however, he couldn't bring himself to speak of her death that freely. Not yet.

"Well, it's early yet. We would like to speak to him," Jim said. "We will be in touch if anything noteworthy comes of it."

Jim and Dan walked back to the front door with Tom accompanying them. The three men stopped at the door and shook hands.

"Listen, there is a memorial service for Ashley tonight. We had to make it family only because of all the media interest, but if either of you are interested you're welcome to come. Don't feel obligated though. I know if it was me I wouldn't want to be there." Tom paused and looked away for a second. "I don't want to be there now," he continued quietly.

"Thank you, I'll certainly try to be there," said Jim. "Do you guys still have someone to help you out? This is the first time I've seen you alone and we can arrange for someone to come by if you like."

"No, uh, Mark will be back. He just went home for a bit to see his family. Thank you though." With that Jim and Dan headed back to their office.

Almost as if he had been watching patiently and waiting for their arrival back at the station, Paul jumped up from his desk and walked quickly to Jim and Dan's desk cluster before they even had a chance to sit down.

"Jesus Christ, Bedard, give me a minute to sit down, will you? You're like a little kid, I told you that you could come, just be patient."

"That's not it. There may be a slight problem with our trip to Davie." Paul said anxiously. "Did either of you read the newspaper this morning or watch the news last night?" Both Jim and Dan shook their heads no. Paul handed Jim the morning's edition of *The Palm Beach Post*. There, under the bold printed headline, "POSSIBLE STRANGLER SUSPECT," was a picture of Louis Bradford. The very same picture Jim had just shown Lisa Wooten. "His mother was the one who was killed the other day. That's why his name sounded familiar to you."

Jim and Dan paused for a moment to take it all in. The initial surprise that their case was yet again linked to another investigation rendered each of them speechless. Then the logistics of what this meant for their investigation set in.

"Who does it say the investigating agency is?" Jim asked pensively.

"It lists the taskforce as investigating it, but there is a quote from a supervisor at the Broward County Sheriff's Office also." Jim immediately flipped through the yellowed cards of his rolodex. He began dialing just as Sergeant Phillips joined them, anxiously awaiting the outcome of Jim's call.

After reaching the supervisor listed in the newspaper article, Jim was given the name and phone number of the lead investigating officer for the Anne Bradford murder. "Holy shit I know this guy." Jim said aloud after he hung up. "Jorge Salazar, I worked with him in some gambling ring taskforce years ago. Nice guy, kind of quiet. Hopefully I can get somewhere with him." Jim knew he needed to be delicate. If there was evidence of Louis's involvement in the South Florida Strangler killings, enough to warrant him being called a suspect, he may have to back off of Louis for a while. All he wanted was to talk to him, to get a feel for him. He desperately hoped that would still be possible.

Jim dialed Jorge's number. The two men exchanged pleasantries and caught up briefly. Jorge told Jim he had just spoken to the doctor who had performed his mother's surgery and laughed about the coincidence that Jim was now calling him. Jim looked up at the three men surrounding him and nodded as if to indicate there would be no problems, which excited them. Jim finally decided to get around to the actual reason for his call. "Listen, Jorge, we had a little girl who was kidnapped on Saturday and murdered and one of our suspects is in your neck of the woods."

"Let me know what I can do to help. I'm a little busy with this but I can get some of our guys to help you." Jorge said back, not realizing what Jim's ultimate request was going to be.

"Well, turns out our suspect is your suspect, too." There was no response. Jim decided to continue. "Louis Bradford was seen at the Boca Towne Center Mall during the time our girl and her mother were there. He even interacted with her. He left shortly before them and out of the same entrance. We need to speak with him. We think he waited for them in the parking lot and followed them home."

"When did you say this was again?" Jorge asked, sounding confused.

"Saturday."

"Jim, I gotta be honest with you, I don't think he's your guy. I mean, he fits perfectly as this serial killer. He kills older women, that's his M.O. Not young children. Do you have any physical evidence that would link him to this?" Jorge was teetering on the edge of enlisting Jim's assistance. He knew in his heart that Louis was not Jim's guy. However, if Jim had some kind of evidence, enough to obtain a search warrant for Louis's apartment and car he would allow Jim to conduct his investigation and gather evidence, which he could also use for his case.

"He's a sex offender for molesting a young girl. No, we don't have any physical evidence right now or we would already have a search warrant," Jim shot back as the conversation began taking a less cordial turn.

"Yes, but that was a long time ago. His first time acting out. Other serial killers started out the same way. Shawcross, for example. I'm telling you he fits perfectly as our guy. He wouldn't be both. That just doesn't happen. You know that just doesn't happen." Jorge was disappointed that Jim could not assist him in getting into Louis's apartment, however, he also felt in some way vindicated that he had the right guy.

"All right, I get that, but we still have to speak to him, you understand. I'm only calling you as a courtesy. We are going to talk with him either way." Jim's voice became gradually more agitated.

"I'm sorry, Jim, you know that's not a good idea. It could jeopardize our whole case. He's a huge flight risk as it is. Do you really want to be the one to screw this up over a theory with no evidence to support it? This is the biggest case in South Florida since both of us have been cops. I know you, you're a good detective, you don't want to do something foolish like that." Jorge's tone was calm yet sharp. He wasn't going to be bullied into letting Jim spook his prime suspect into hiding.

"This guy raped and murdered a child, you don't care about that? You're going to let him go free?" Jim was angry now and throwing anything he could at Jorge, trying to guilt him into agreeing to the interview.

"Trust me, he is not going free. Just be patient. Once we make an arrest and he is in custody I will call you and you can ask him whatever you like. Or, if, by chance, something changes and he is not our guy I'll call you right away. But I don't expect it to. I'm sorry, man. I don't know what else to tell you."

"Yeah, thanks a lot." Jim said as he hung up the phone in a huff. He looked down at the phone for a second trying to catch his breath and calm a bit, then he looked up at the group who eagerly awaited a response. "Forget it, this guy's an asshole. He's not gonna help us. Chris, can't you make some calls? I mean, I just wanna talk to this guy, that's all." Jim was desperate.

"We got no evidence, Jim. I know he seems promising, but we can't put him in the little girl's neighborhood. Go re-canvass, show the neighbors his pictures. But for now we have to back off." Sergeant Phillips gave a sympathetic look to his detectives, then walked back into his office.

CHAPTER 16

As the days passed Jim and Dan tried their hardest to link Louis Bradford to Ashley's murder but were unable to come up with any physical evidence to do it. Tips continued to pour in and they would follow up on them as well, but most were fruitless. They continued to look into Angela, but eventually they came to the realization that she wasn't involved in Ashley's kidnapping or murder and cleared her as a suspect. They seemed to be in a holding pattern, just waiting for the go ahead to speak with Louis Bradford, who at this point, was their only suspect. Of course, he was also the prime suspect in the South Florida Strangler case, to which they now paid close attention.

Each day with no news regarding the South Florida Strangler, Jim became more convinced that Jorge had nothing. The more time passed the more the case frustrated him. Jim and Dan both had attended Ashley's services, at the funeral home, the church, and the cemetery. Jim revisited the torturous thoughts of his own daughters and again struggled with the different emotions that came with it. But that was over now; Ashley was at rest, though he hesitated to think of it as such. Little girls shouldn't be laid "to rest," he thought. He pictured old, tired people passing away when he heard that phrase, which he had heard a lot over the past several days. Little girls should be full of energy. They should be dancing, running, living life. Like his daughters were.

The case was still a hotbed of discussion in the media and so he knew he would be allowed to continue to work it as his one and only assignment for a little while longer, however, the time would soon come when he would have to push it aside and begin a new project. He became angry at the thought. He knew that it could be months or longer before the taskforce made their case against Bradford and arrested him or decided he wasn't their man. And at that point, who knew if they would be able to gather enough evidence from whatever trampled crime scenes were left over. He couldn't bear the thought of letting this case go unsolved. But, unfortunately, for the time being, he would have to simply wait while his prime suspect walked free, knowing he may never catch him.

It had been one week since Ashley's abduction. One week since the Wootens' lives had been "normal." Now they were anything but. Tom now spent a lot of time sitting out on the deck by himself, mainly in the evening when it wasn't too hot.

He had let his business go over the course of the week, closing it down most of the time. But, he realized, despite the fact that he was in no condition to reopen and run it, it would need to continue on, and so Tom put Rick in charge of all decisions. Kurt continued to work there as well and the two seemed to be doing well without Tom.

The store had become somewhat of a makeshift memorial. Customers, friends, and strangers would stop by and drop off cards or stuffed animals in front. Tom had no ambition to go back, and with Rick and Kurt willing to pick up the slack, he had no idea of when he might.

As he sat, a glass of sweet tea on the table beside him, and looked out into the darkness of the moonless evening, he recalled moments he had shared with his daughter. Like the time she had gotten her head and right arm stuck in between two of the deck pickets. She was about three years old and she was playing with the dog while Tom and Lisa sat at the very same table that Tom's sweet tea now rested on. Apparently she had thought she could fit between the pickets and had wedged herself in good by the time Tom and Lisa were alerted to the situation by a high pitched scream. It took some time, but they were able to wiggle Ashley back out without hurting her or causing any damage to the deck.

Tom smirked as he remembered the scene, which at the time was not so humorous. He envisioned her running in the backyard as he sat there—something she did often—his last real memory of her. He reflected on that moment, only a week ago, and how, even then, his subconscious had cried out to him to drink it up. She was doing nothing really significant at the time, just running and chasing the dog. It wasn't a major milestone such as her first steps or first word or first day of preschool. But for some reason he thought to himself at the time that it was important and to enjoy and remember it. And now he was glad he had.

While Tom sat alone on the deck, illuminated by only one small light that shined over the table and chairs, Lisa had already been in bed for hours. That was the way she had spent most of her days since Ashley's death. She had never been good at dealing with grief, and thankfully, to this point in her life, she really hadn't had to. She had been taking a steady diet of sleeping pills and oxycodone since Monday and had begun to feel as if she couldn't survive without them. She didn't want to feel the pain that overcame her like an avalanche if she was raw and unprotected.

She was in an almost zombie-like state at the funeral and even then she didn't think she could go on. Every word that hit her ears brought pain and sorrow. But the cemetery was worse. She wanted to die herself when she was there, and felt like at any moment she would. She couldn't begin to imagine how she would overcome this state she was in. Getting back to her old self seemed impossible. She couldn't escape the thought that her daughter, her flesh and blood, was in a box under six feet of dirt. The thought almost suffocated her. What if she was cold down there? What if she was scared? What if it rained? They were torturous, the thoughts that would plague her mind. And so she took pills to make the thoughts go away, or at least temporarily quiet them down.

Mark sat on the living room couch, his makeshift bed and bedroom, and turned on the television. He was trying to be the glue that kept everything together, but he was faltering. It had been a hard week for him as well. Not only did he have the services and memorials to attend, but he also had to look after two people who were destroyed inside. He had hired an attorney after Tom reluctantly agreed to it. The family had been inundated with phone calls from news stations and papers looking for interviews. Tom had told him from the beginning he did not want to speak publicly. He just wanted to let the police do their jobs.

As he flipped through the channels he stopped on one of the national news stations. He looked in amazement at what the headline at the bottom of the screen read. There, in bold print, was, "BOCA RATON GIRL KIDNAPPED AND MURDERED WHERE ARE THE PARENTS?" Mark leaned forward and turned up the volume. The show was a crime talk show, hosted by a former federal prosecutor named Amber Gentrey. On this particular episode of the show there were two other people in a three-way split-screen debating the circumstances surrounding Ashley's death. The photo issued to police of Ashley, as well as a few others of the entire family would occasionally cover the screen as the three people debated. Mark was stunned. He had seen some local news stories on Ashley's death and read about it in the newspapers, but it had never crossed his mind that it would be covered nationally on such a well-known television show.

"So, where is the family here, Murphy? It's been a week since their daughter's death and we haven't heard word one from any of them. Are they hiding something? Families always try to solicit support and tips by issuing statements and having fundraisers, especially when the child is kidnapped first." The host shouted, looking into the camera the entire time. Her blonde hair rested neatly at her shoulders. Her blue eyes, set in a fixed gaze, and appeared calm even though her nostrils flared.

A man of middle age, shown only from the chest up, dressed in a black suit and red tie, took up one part of the three-way split-screen. His hair only existed in small patches on the side of his head and his mustache matched its auburn color. The name "Francis Murphy" flashed briefly under his face and written under that were the words "High Profile Defense Attorney in Miami, FL."

"Amber, this attack on the family is way out of line," he shouted back. "I mean, people deal with grief differently. There is no written rule that states that families have to come forward and make a public plea. The girl's father has an ironclad alibi and her mother is the one who contacted police. Also, police have given the indication the little girl was sexually assaulted, now come on, just because they aren't mugging it up in front of the cameras doesn't mean they were involved or know more than they are telling police."

The other occupant of the split screen was an attractive brunette who looked to be considerably younger than the host. Her brown eyes looked intently into the camera, and occasionally she nodded, both yes and no, while the other two debaters were speaking. She, too, could only be seen from the chest up and her white blouse was unbuttoned just enough to reveal a silver heart necklace that sparkled as it rested in the divot of her collarbone. Under her face briefly flashed "Nicole Kirkman" and under that read "Reporter, *Sun Sentinel.*" Now it was her turn to chime in.

"Amber, I do agree to an extent with Frank. Families have a right to grieve in private if they choose and it in no way reflects guilt or innocence, but it is peculiar behavior at the least that not even a statement has been read. This is a high profile case in our area, and in some circles it has stolen attention away from the serial killer that is also striking in our midst. The family has to understand that people are interested and could possibly aid in the apprehension of their daughter's killer. Also, Frank's argument that sexual assault excludes the family by default is ridiculous. Remember Jean Benet Ramsey was sexually assaulted and the family was the top suspect for years."

"That's a terrible point, Kirkman, the family was excluded years later and that investigation was plagued by shoddy police work," shouted the host.

"I'm just saying, it happens," snapped Nicole, looking a bit embarrassed.

"All right, well, we have a caller on the line who claims to have had an affair with Tom Wooten, the little girl's father. Angela, are you there?" Amber shouted, looking directly into the television. Mark couldn't believe what he was seeing or hearing. This was a nationally televised program; it had millions of viewers. The fact that his niece's murder was being discussed was surprising enough, but the fact that his brother and sister-in-law were being accused of withholding information in her murder was shocking and upsetting. And now a woman was going to broadcast her claims of having an affair with Tom so the whole world could hear—it was more than he could take.

Mark stood up and turned off the television. He turned and faced the deck where he could see the back of Tom's head lit up as he sat in the deck chair. Angry, hurt, surprised, Mark stormed out on to the deck not really knowing what he was going to say or do. Tom looked up at him, startled.

"Oh, hey, I thought you had fallen asleep. What time is it?" Tom asked sounding groggy.

"We need to talk, Tom," Mark said in an anxious tone. "Do you know what is being said about you in the press? On television? National television, actually." Tom looked confused, but said nothing. "You have to give the media something, you have to at least issue a statement, through the lawyer I hired, something." Tom just shook his head and turned away as Mark pleaded. "Tom, people think you and Lisa were involved, like that Jean Benet Ramsey case. They at least think you know something about it."

"Let them think what they want, I don't care," Tom snapped back. He was trying to remain calm and keep his voice down, but the anger and hurt was beginning to boil over.

"You don't care? What about asking for the public's help? Every time a child is killed or kidnapped I always see the family on TV, holding posters or pictures, wearing ribbons, asking for help. Asking for tips, pleading with the killer to come forward."

"The police are doing that. I don't want to interfere. They know what they are doing. Jim and Dan are good guys, they were at Ashley's services, and I trust them." Tom continued to stare ahead blankly as he spoke with Mark, who was still standing slightly behind his right shoulder.

"What about starting some type of fund or foundation in Ashley's honor? People do that all the time, too. People take up a cause and petition the governor for law changes, they say these things change their lives, make them want to help change things so other kids don't get hurt." Mark's voice was starting to fade. He was throwing out every idea he could think of in an attempt to help his brother. Tom was still his idol, and to see him in such pain and then to hear his name tarnished was agony for him. He wanted desperately for Tom to do something, to stop the public humiliation television shows such as the one he had just been watching would soon bring him.

But Tom had had enough; his breaking point had been reached. He stood up quickly and faced his younger brother.

"What the hell do you watch all day? The Kidnapped Children's Network? How many people do you actually know who have actually gone through this? Huh? I'm guessing two!" Tom took a deep breath to regain his composure and lowered his voice. He moved in closer to Mark and spoke intensely, though his voice was only a whisper, tears beginning to well up in his eyes.

"I don't give a shit about any other kids getting hurt. My daughter is dead. Nothing is going to bring her back. Nothing is going to make me whole again. No foundation, no ribbons, nothing. Do I look like John fucking Walsh? I have no causes now. She was my cause. She was the reason I worked hard to make money, for her. That was my cause. I'm not going to be out there begging the person who took her away from me to turn himself in, cause it's not going to happen. I'm not going to give that piece of shit the satisfaction of seeing my tears. Him or anyone else. No one can tell me how to grieve for my daughter." Tom stopped, his chin quivering a bit, his eyes wide, staring deeply into Mark's.

Mark looked down briefly, then looked back into Tom's eyes. He felt badly that he had provoked Tom in such a way. These were emotions he had never seen from his brother before. But he knew he needed to press further, for Tom's own good and the good of his family.

"There is something else, Tom. A woman named Angela was on television just now claiming to the whole world you had an affair with her." Tom closed his eyes and kept them shut as he stood in front of Mark. "I'm not going to preach to you about marriage, or even ask you if it's true. But if it is, you should get in front of this. At least tell Lisa, I mean my God, in her state if she found out from a reporter or the news—" Mark shook his head as he abruptly stopped. Tom took a deep breath and opened his eyes. They were no longer wide and alert. They now seemed tired and worn down.

"What do you want from me? Huh? I'm a bad guy, Mark, I'm not the person you think I am. I've made plenty of mistakes, and now my family is paying for them. What's left of it, anyway."

"Well, are you going to tell her?"

"I don't know . . . she's so out of it she wouldn't understand. She would be destroyed worse than she is now."

"You've got to tell her, Tom. And you have to watch her with those prescriptions. She's taking too many. Take it from me, I've been through it. If you don't help her she's going to become addicted."

"That's her problem," Tom said in a cold, uncaring tone while looking away.

Mark was visibly taken aback by this comment and he shook his head from side to side quickly as if to rattle the words around in his skull to make sure he had heard them correctly.

"WHAT? What the hell do you mean, 'that's her problem'? She's your wife. She's all you have now. She is hurting worse than anyone I've ever seen and she needs you to keep her from a lifetime of addiction and dependency on things that don't make her hurt so bad. She will never deal with this if she is doped up all the time like she has been."

Tom just stood there for a moment looking away from Mark. He took a deep breath and nodded his head yes, then patted his brother on the right shoulder. It seemed to be enough to satisfy Mark, even though nothing had really been said to that effect, and he lumbered back inside and plopped down on the couch. Tom had no intention at all of doing anything Mark had suggested; he was just too worn down to discuss it any further.

He had always relished the role of mentor to Mark. He couldn't open up to his younger brother. To tell him his fears about all the mistakes he had made. He couldn't tell him that he only cared about himself and not his ailing wife. He had begun resenting Lisa for Ashley's death, though he hadn't said so to anyone and had tried not to show it. He actually preferred her heavily medicated as she had been all week because he could be alone and didn't have to deal with her grief as well as his. Her current supply of oxycodone and the sleeping pills would both last her for about a month, assuming she took them as prescribed.

Tom didn't know how long she planned to be medicated and he didn't really care to know. He was just in a state of being. He was just there. He did not want to think about the future or how he would overcome what had happened. He did not want to look out for his wife. He didn't care what was being said about him and what his reputation would be. He just wanted to exist in each moment, no more, no less.

Tom exhaled loudly and sat back down in his chair, his empty gaze returning to the yard. Visions of a strawberry blonde chasing a small dog and giggling resumed. He raised the glass of sweet tea to his lips, then slowly lowered it back to the table.

CHAPTER 17

"Make yourself comfortable. You're going to be here awhile," the detective said as he took off a pair of handcuffs and guided his prisoner to the chair in front of him. There sat a young black man, roughly twenty-two years old, in a dirty white wifebeater and black shorts. He sat looking down at the table in front of him, his hands placed on either side of his head under his thick, short dreadlocks. The detective sat on the other side of the small table in a similar chair. The room wasn't a typical interrogation room from television. It was small, with similarly small furnishings. The square table was located in the back right hand corner and only two small folding chairs accommodated it, one on either side. Two other chairs were left unoccupied against a wall and above them hung the obligatory two way mirror.

Detective Chris Cantore was dressed in a white, long-sleeved dress shirt with a black tie. He had jet black hair that was loosely combed forward and mussed up so that the points formed by his hair product were going in different directions. His brown eyes were fixed on the young man he had before him and he leaned his head down as if trying to look under the dreadlocks that covered his prisoner's face. "So this is what we got, Jemile. I got you dealing coke and heroin to undercover police officers. Not once, not twice, but nine times. Nine times. That's gonna set you back, my friend. Oh yeah, and then, and this is one of my favorite parts. Not my favorite part, that's coming, but one of my favorite parts. So then, when we go to pick you up, you have a crack pipe in your sock and a gun on you. A stolen gun." Detective Cantore smiled as he continued to look at the top of the dreadlocked head. "You want to say anything to that?"

"I told you I was holding that gun for someone else, it wasn't even mine. And there ain't no way I sold nothin to an undercover cop." Jemile looked up for the first time with anger in his eyes. "Crooked ass cops probably made up the story just to try to put me in jail," he said as he looked back down.

"You know, I thought you might say that, so . . ." Detective Cantore stood up abruptly from his seat. He wheeled over a television which sat on a large podium with a DVD player on the shelf underneath it and placed it in front of the table so Jemile could see it. "Now this is my favorite part," he said as he turned on the television.

As the television picture came into view, Jemile could see what looked like a news broadcast. The screen was frozen, but clearly depicted a woman facing the camera holding a microphone. She was on a street and behind her right shoulder, in the background, Jemile could see several people on the sidewalk.

"Now watch this closely," the detective said as he hit the play button. The reporter began speaking about a murder that had been committed in the house she stood in front of and the camera panned over to the house then back to her. Jemile's right leg began to bounce up and down as he bit his lower lip. The reporter continued, saying that the murder was most likely linked to the South Florida Strangler. Detective Cantore hit the pause button and the screen froze once again.

"Now that you have just a touch of the back story on this, here's a better version of this disc. This exact screen, actually. We have some cool toys that allow us to zoom and focus and all that good stuff." Detective Cantore replaced the disc currently in the DVD player with a different one. It appeared to be the same screen that had been paused on the previous disc, however, it was zoomed in over the reporter's right shoulder to the people on the sidewalk.

The people were fairly clear, even though they were slightly pixilated. Jemile recognized himself instantly but remained silent. He stood there, on the sidewalk looking around, facing the camera, obviously unaware he was being recorded. His facial features were difficult to distinguish, but the dreadlocks were perfectly clear. From off camera came another black male who walked up to him and the two slapped hands. Jemile pulled him in for a brief embrace and the man continued on his way. The disc stopped playing again.

"Now, let's watch that again in slow motion." Detective Cantore restarted the disc from the beginning, this time, in slow motion. The image of what appeared to be a hand reaching around the back of the black male Jemile had pulled in for a hug was now visible with the video slowed. That hand, presumably Jemile's, could now be seen slipping something into the back pants pocket of his visitor. The black male then pulled his shirt down over his back pants pocket and walked away. Detective Cantore stopped the recording again and sat back down, smiling at Jemile, who was leaned back in his chair with his head up and arms crossed. His gaze, though it was on the table in front of him, appeared to be far off. He nervously bit his lower lip. "Do you recognize those guys? The guys on the second disc?"

"Nope," Jemile said sharply still gazing at the table in front of him.

"Well, the first guy, the one in the white tank top looking toward the camera, well, that guy is you, Jemile. Your wardrobe doesn't change much does it?" Jemile didn't respond. "And that other guy, the one you pulled in for that warm embrace, did you recognize him?"

"Nope."

"Hmmm . . . you must hug a lot of guys like that then. Pull them in nice and tight. I bet you blew on his ear when you pulled him in, didn't you? Maybe I've got this all wrong, maybe you weren't dealing drugs, maybe you just like touching dudes. Getting them all close like that. I bet you—"

"MAN, IT AIN'T LIKE THAT! I AIN'T NO FAG!" Jemile interrupted in an explosion. Detective Cantore just smiled back at him.

"All right, Jemile, just to refresh your memory a bit," Detective Cantore opened a folder and pulled out a booking photo of a black male that looked similar to the one in the video with Jemile. "You know this guy, don't you?"

"Nope." Despite his defiance, Jemile knew he was in big trouble. He knew there was no way out of this. Jemile had been dealing drugs since he was fourteen years old. He had had a few brushes with the law but nothing ever resulted in jail time.

"So you're probably wondering why I'm still talking to you at this point and you're not already in a jail cell getting used to your new pad for the next twenty years. Well, because it's your lucky day, I guess. See, normally I could give a shit about a drug dealing thug like you, but today, well, I'm going to give you the opportunity to help yourself out a little bit. I want your supplier. You know, your buddy from the disc." Detective Cantore pointed to the booking photo that still lay on the table. "I want him on tape. You know, better than this one. I know you get your stuff from this guy. Slipping that envelope of money in his back pocket, I gotta give it to you, that was smooth. Thank God for video manipulation. Anyway, we know he goes by the street name Prince. His real name is Tashawn Jordan. You're going to get me Prince on tape discussing his operation and who he gets his shit from. See that's who we want, and that's how this works. Hell, he can't be that smart of a guy either, agreeing to meet you on the street like that when there is a homicide investigation going on two doors down. It gives me hope that you can pull this off. You give us Prince, he gives us his guy. If you do that, well, then maybe some of these more serious charges go away."

Jemile smiled at Detective Cantore, flashing his gold teeth. "You crazy right? You think I'm giving you shit? First off, Prince ain't gonna tell me any of that shit, and he sure as hell ain't gonna give you anything. And you expect me to wear a wire? He'd smell that shit a mile away. He'd cap my ass. Ain't no way."

"Jemile, maybe you're not understanding the situation you're in. A fully loaded, stolen gun was found on your person. A crack pipe was found on your person. Detectives are going to testify you sold them felony drugs nine times. You're going away for a long time. This is you're only shot to avoid that. You give us Prince, those things get reduced to maybe a misdemeanor and probation. And besides, what's Prince gonna think when we show him this video? And then we tell him all the charges we got on you, you think he's gonna trust that you won't roll over on him? I'm sure he's got friends in the can. Guys that would be willing to shut you up for him before your trial."

"You ain't gonna show him this shit! You can't do that!" Jemile leaned forward in his chair as he shouted. He knew it would mean a target on his back if Prince thought there was a chance he had or would flip. He leaned back with his arms crossed again. He tried to consider what his legitimate options were. If he gave up Prince he knew he would be facing a death penalty on the streets. It wasn't an option. He shook his head from side to side again.

"You know what, screw this. Time's up," Detective Cantore said as he stood up. "Get up, Jemile, get up and put your hands behind your back. Hope you enjoyed your last day in the hood cause you won't be seeing it for a long time." Detective Cantore came around to the other side of the table.

"Wait!" Jemile shouted as he leaned in his chair away from the approaching detective. "Just wait a second."

"You gonna give me Prince?"

"No, but I can give you something else. If I give you Prince I'm dead. But I know other stuff." He looked desperately at the detective in hopes he would have the opportunity to bargain for his freedom.

Detective Cantore looked at Jemile pensively. He didn't care about anything Jemile had to say other than information about Prince, but something about Jemile's desperate plea made him curious.

"OK, Jemile, I'll bite," he said as he went back to other side of the table and sat down.

A week had passed since Anne Bradford's death and Jorge and the taskforce still had not gathered enough evidence to obtain a search warrant for her son's apartment or his vehicle. Jorge was confident that Louis had not fled the area as of yet, even though twenty four hour surveillance on him had been discontinued two days ago. Someone drove past the house each day and the car was always in the same spot. Even when an officer was sitting in front they never saw Louis do anything but go between the garage and the main house.

The police had also confiscated a large sum of money from Anne's bedroom during a search of her home after her murder, as well as frozen her bank accounts. Jorge was trying to make the decision to flee, and life in general, as difficult as possible on Louis.

Jorge was certain that something that had been collected from the garage or the main house would come back from the crime lab and link the other South Florida Strangler victims to Louis, and then they would have enough not only for a search warrant, but an arrest. He was hoping for the crime lab's report on those things today. What had Jorge most anxious was the small amount of DNA successfully collected from the back of Anne's neck. He had high hopes a profile could be extracted from the samples obtained. If it could, he knew it would be a match to Louis.

As the hours ticked away he found it hard to focus on anything other than the pending results, so he, John, and Kristin decided to go to a nice lunch to ease the tension a bit. While there, Jorge received a phone call on his cell phone. The call was brief, but Jorge's reaction to it was telling to the other members of the lunch party. They assumed this was it.

"What is it?" Kristin asked, seeing through Jorge's attempts to hide his excitement.

"Gonna have to wrap up your meals and eat them later. We gotta meet with Narcotics ASAP." Jorge said as he motioned for the waitress.

"Narcotics, why? I thought we was waitin on a call from Forensics?" John said looking confused as he packed up his lunch.

"We are, but Narcotics just called me, said they got a guy in custody saying he has some info on the South Florida Strangler. They said it sounds legit." The three hurried out of the restaurant, each carrying a Styrofoam container.

Jorge, John, and Kristin all pulled chairs up to the table across from Jemile, who by now had a can of cola in front of him. Detective Cantore leaned against the two way mirror and prompted Jemile to tell the detectives what he had told him. Jemile took a sip of his soda and began speaking in a slow, calm tone, much the opposite of how he had spoken in the bulk of his interrogation with

Detective Cantore. "The house where that lady got killed, the old lady, I've seen stuff there."

"What kind of stuff do you mean? Just to be clear, you are talking about 320 J Street, the Bradford residence, correct?" Jorge asked, tape recorder on the table in front of him.

"Yeah, 320 J Street, a few houses down from me. I lived in that house all my life and long as I been there she lived there with her son, the fat dude. Weird guy, guess he was a child molester back in the day, least that's what my grandma told me. Anyway, she always told me to stay away from him, you know, when I was younger cause he older than me you know, he like forty." He took another sip.

"Did he ever try to interact with you?" Jorge prodded.

"Nah, never really. But she say back when my aunt was young she had a dog and he had caught the dog in some kind of trap he had in his yard and tried to steal it. He tried to take it into the garage with him but my pops caught him before he could shut the door and beat his ass good. She said he used to have lots of traps in the yard he'd catch animals in. I never forgot that story, cause it weird right? Stealing a dog from your neighbor? He'd have to be a dumbass to think my aunt wouldn't have known he had it. She would have seen it if he tried to keep it for himself."

Jorge was beginning to get excited with the minimal information he had received so far. Though it did not incriminate Louis in any crime, it gave some background information on who he was. He let Jemile continue, in hopes he had some actual usable information in reference to the South Florida Strangler killings.

"So anyway, I always kept an eye out for him. He was known around the neighborhood as a child molester and a weirdo. He didn't really come out much, never stepped off his property unless he was in his car. He made his moms walk to the bus stop, but he drove everywhere. Sometimes when he'd come home, some of us would sneak over and peek down his driveway to see what he was doing. He'd be carrying laundry out his car all wrapped in a blanket. Sometimes he'd even talk to the shit. We always thought it was weird. Sometimes we'd sneak over at night when we'd hear the garage door go up and see him bringing laundry out to his car wrapped in the same blanket. It would be late, too, like two, three in the morning. Who does they laundry at night? Some weird shit, going to a Laundromat at two in the morning. But the weirdest thing was, few times years back, I'd be out on the porch at three, four in the morning and I'd hear sounds coming from his backyard. You know, the street quiet at that time so I could hear it clearly. I snuck over once and the motherfucker digging in the backyard. I couldn't see what he was digging exactly, it was dark, but I could see him and the shovel would catch the light from the street. We used to joke he was a serial killer, but this was way back, you know, before this serial killer shit came out in the papers. Then, couple nights before his moms got killed, at least a couple nights before y'all showed up and found her, I was walking in front of they house and I heard him screaming at her, calling her stupid and selfish and shit. I stopped to listen for a few minutes. It was crazy. Dude just went off on her. That pretty much it, he your guy, now what y'all gonna do for me?"

He took a sip of his soda, his swagger returning. He felt confident he'd saved himself from prison and the wrath of Prince by giving them this information, which was all true and accurate. When Jemile had seen all the police at the Bradford home on the day Anne's body was discovered he had thought to himself that the police had finally found the bodies Louis had buried in the backyard. He chuckled about it, but part of him felt there was a possibility that's what was going on over there. He had always joked, but never actually linked him to the serial killer striking in the area until someone had said it while they all sat on the porch a few days after Anne's body was discovered. He never would have volunteered the information he had just given, but it had been in the back of his mind that he might be able to use it as a bargaining chip if he had to. He actually had forgotten about it until he saw the video of the newscast.

"Write everything you just told me down and if it turns out to be legit, we will work with Detective Cantore and the State Attorney's Office on your charges." Jorge slid a piece of paper and a pen across the table and Jemile began to write.

Jorge now had enough, he was certain, for a search warrant of Louis Bradford's apartment and car. He wrote up the warrant himself and hurried it to a judge, who approved it without a problem. He assembled a team of forensic personnel, uniformed officers, and members of the SWAT team. This was a man who was the prime suspect as a serial killer; Jorge was taking no chances. He didn't have enough to charge Louis yet, but he had enough to bring him in for questioning once again. And once in for questioning he could detain Louis until the results of the hair analysis was in and the DNA retrieved from the back of Anne's neck was matched to Louis's profile, which was already in the system as part of his sex offender status. Finally, the team had a plan of attack and was on its way.

Because the setup to Louis's apartment was so unique, it posed a nightmare to the SWAT team as far as making entry and bringing Louis out. There was a small window in the front of the apartment that allowed Louis to view the driveway leading up to the front of the garage. The team decided they would cut through the property next door and enter the backyard instead of walking down the driveway. That way they could access the garage door from the side instead of the front so even if Louis happened to be looking out the window, he wouldn't see them coming until they were there.

The next problem they faced was getting the garage door open. The only entrance was a pull down garage door that had the capability of locking. It was an older model, not electric, and so they brought a tool with them that would punch the lock if necessary. One team member would be positioned across the street from the garage with a clear view of the window and would be trained on it with a rifle, ready to fire if he felt it necessary to protect the officers making entry. There was also the chance Louis was inside the main house by the time they arrived and so they positioned officers around the front and back doors. The apartment was their main concern, however, since they knew he spent the majority of his time there. Everyone knew there was no one hundred percent safe way to go about this. There were multiple safety risks involved.

The team slowly made their way to the garage door. Four SWAT officers went first, with Jorge, Kristin, and John waiting in the backyard for entry to be made. As the first officer grabbed the garage door handle the tension grew, anxiety built. This was a very violent man, and now his back was to the wall. He hadn't been seen in days, he could have been anticipating this moment, preparing for it, barricading himself in. They knew that once inside the garage that was not enough. The tactical nightmare continued with the entrance to Louis's actual apartment. They would try to coax him down voluntarily, but if he did not come, they knew they would have to go up the ladder after him.

The garage door handle turned; it was left unlocked. The lead officer looked back and motioned to the other officers that it was time, the door was going up, get ready. In a flash the door went up and the officers rushed into the garage, guns drawn. Jorge waited to make sure there was no gunfire before he made his way in.

His gun was still drawn as he walked purposefully into the garage, trying to understand what was being said by the officers inside. He heard them clearly, they were cursing, they were angry. But what did it mean? He made his way slowly to the back corner where the SWAT team had congregated, his gun lowered to the ground. Then he understood their anger and frustration. He understood because his was far greater. He holstered his weapon and turned away, putting both hands behind his head. "God damn it!" He screamed. John and Kristin ran into the garage past him. They froze just as he had.

The stench overwhelmed each of them first as they entered. Just based on that alone they should have known what their eyes were going to see. Among the clutter of the garage, near the entrance hatch to the apartment above, which was open with the ladder pulled down, Louis lay face down on the cement. Flies and other insects swarmed him; his extremities had begun turning darker shades. Around his neck was a noose, made from old rope that had probably been in the garage since his father was alive. The rope had snapped a short distance from the hangman's knot with the other end still hanging down from the apartment above. The rope had apparently given way under Louis's weight, but it appeared to have done so post mortem as a fall from such a short distance would not have caused his death.

Next to his body, on a stack of boxes, was a note. It had been folded up and placed in an envelope, but not sealed. Jorge pulled the note carefully from the envelope with gloved hands and read its contents. It was simple and short, hardly the confession one would expect at the end of such a monstrous life. It read, "Mom, I'm sorry." No details on his crimes, no description of what he was sorry for. Jorge felt that the note, though vague, and the following suicide were admissions of guilt for what he had done to his mother, and in a way he was right.

The crime scene investigation would go deep into the night. The small apartment was indeed a treasure trove of DNA evidence as Jorge had suspected it would be. The car once shared by Louis and his mother also yielded DNA evidence, as well as a police scanner radio. The delicate brushes and swabs of the interior forensic investigation eventually gave way to the brute strength of a backhoe, which would be used in the exterior investigation. Jemile had told of digging being done, and even though all the South Florida Strangler victims' bodies had been found in their homes, Jorge thought perhaps there were more victims no one was aware of. Maybe this was how he started; burying his victims in the backyard.

Sure enough as the digging progressed in the small yard, multiple skeletons were found. A large amount of animal bones were found, but scattered among them were three human skulls. Jorge looked on in amazement and excitement. But as he approached the skulls he noticed a problem. He was no pathologist, but he knew what the size of an adult skull should have looked like, and the three before him did not match up. They were too small. He puzzled over it. They couldn't belong to children. It didn't fit the strangler's pattern. He wouldn't just switch like that. Then he thought of Jim Brekenridge and the conversation they had had days before. Amidst his panic he tried to convince himself that Louis could still be his guy. He needed to hold judgment until the DNA results came in.

CHAPTER 18

About two weeks had passed since Carlos had taken Anne's life. To him it still seemed like yesterday. He replayed that evening over and over in his head and was extremely pleased with its outcome. He was certain he had left no traceable evidence behind and would continue to go on undetected. He had reveled in the media sensationalism of his crimes. Discussed in the newspapers or on television every day since Anne's murder, he was known only as the South Florida Strangler, of course. It had scratched his itch for the time being. He continued on with work as he normally would: performed a few surgeries, saw several patients. It was as if he was back to being a normal person. It was Dr. Jekyll who was now present.

He had tried to spend more time with Julia, though she had not had a lot of time for him. She would tell him she had plans with friends or had picked up some modeling jobs, something she did quite frequently, and he would end up spending his time alone instead. He never blamed her for it and certainly never expected that anything was going on behind his back. With his being away from the house so much, either with work or with his extracurricular activities, he had encouraged her to go out and be social in his absence. And now he understood that he couldn't just say, "I'm done killing people for a while, I demand you spend time with me while I am free."

Julia, of course, continued to exploit Carlos's unwavering love and trust in her. Over the course of the past few weeks, when Carlos had been so desperate to make up for lost time, she was meeting up with her boyfriend. She had finally gotten through to him and the two began spending a lot of time together. Julia had all but stopped seeing other men, at least during that time, and just spent time with him. Each time she would come back home to Carlos she felt trapped. Trapped by his money. Trapped by her lavish desires. She had felt this way often and for some time, but the feeling of ensnarement was becoming greater and greater.

Carlos sat in his home office reading a magazine at his desk. Julia had gone to a nail salon to get a manicure with Vikki, so Carlos took some time to study up on some new surgical procedures discussed in the current issue of a medical journal he subscribed to. As he read his mind began to wander. He thought back to some of the news reports he had seen on television about his alter ego. He beamed as he recalled how they described him as extremely intelligent and methodical. He recalled his run-ins with police and how he had outsmarted them. First with Rebecca Sullivan, then more recently with the detective investigating Anne Bradford. He felt a sense of pride, a sense of invincibility.

He was just about to unlock his "trophy" drawer when he heard the front door open. Julia was home. His trophies would have to wait to be enjoyed. "Julia, I'm in the office," he shouted from his desk chair. "Let me see those beautiful hands." He went back to reading his magazine, waiting to be interrupted. He could hear her footsteps getting closer as he read until he knew she was standing at the door, so he swiveled his chair and looked up.

A deafening, almost annoyingly loud noise pierced the air, but only for a moment, then there was silence. His chair rocked backward then snapped forward, gently tossing him face first onto the carpeted floor. A sea of red tarnished the once white Berber carpet. Carlos's body slumped on the floor; his buttocks rose slightly toward the ceiling, his knees and what was left of his forehead rested on the carpet, arms tucked beneath his body. Brain and skull covered one of the office walls like an abstract painting punctuated by a single bullet lodged there. The life of yet another monster had come to an abrupt end.

The South Florida Strangler died swiftly, something he had never provided to his victims. He never had to gasp for air as they had. But Carlos's killer had no interest in the serial killer's real crimes. It wasn't a man who sought vengeance for the death of a loved one that had killed Carlos. It was a man who sought to protect someone from Carlos's wrath. It was a man who had listened to tales of abuse and torture until he could take it no longer. It was Julia's boyfriend, Tom Wooten.

As Tom stood in the foyer he felt nothing. He felt empty. No fear, no sense of urgency to get out, nothing. He took a black backpack off his shoulders and opened it up. He took out a pair of navy blue cargo shorts, a t-shirt, and sneakers and changed into them. The khaki pants, blue polo shirt, and dress shoes he had been wearing replaced his new attire in the backpack. He fixed his hair as best he could with his hands and the black Nike ball cap he had been wearing went in to the backpack with the rest of his clothes. He pulled a pair of dark sunglasses out of a side pocket of the backpack and put them on. A slight change in his appearance to help him go undetected after his crime. Though he didn't know it, it was a very similar technique to those used by the man he had just murdered. He opened the front door while still clad in white latex gloves, then closed and locked it. He quickly walked away from the house on the sidewalk, removing the gloves and placing them in his pocket as he did.

The houses in the community where Julia and Carlos lived had quite a distance between them as each property had roughly a half acre of land. Julia and Carlos lived almost on the apex of a curve in the road, and so Tom really only had the neighbors across the street to avoid, at least initially. As Tom walked the mile distance to the exit of the complex, he reflected on how his life had come to this. How he had been driven to murder. How in less than a month's time his life had become unrecognizable.

He met Julia about five months ago. She had been spending some time in Boca Raton on a photo shoot and decided to get her nails done for the occasion, as she often did. She went to a salon that was in the same strip mall as Tom's computer shop. As Julia left the nail salon she noticed the little computer store as she walked by. She had recently been having problems with her laptop and she wondered if they could give her some suggestions on how to fix it. As she entered the store searching for help Tom was sitting at the front desk.

Like most, Tom was immediately struck by Julia's beauty, and she appeared to be equally as interested in him, giving him a seductive smile as she approached. She explained her computer quandary to Tom, who in turn gave her some advice on fixing it. It had indeed been a very minor problem with an easy solution. The two flirted and joked for a while. As Julia reluctantly began her stroll to the door, she turned just as she reached for the handle and asked if Tom wouldn't mind helping her with her computer problems personally. "I know it's a long drive to Coral Gables, but I don't think I can do this on my own. I need someone with experience," she said, punctuating her demand with a sultry emphasis. Tom of course agreed to assist her and gave her a business card with his office telephone number.

A few days later she called and Tom headed out for the "service call." Tom had observed Julia wearing a wedding ring when she had come into the shop, but being married himself, he didn't care. Julia, as she had planned, was alone when Tom arrived and the evening went much the way he had expected and hoped it would, the way other similar service calls had. But there was something different about Julia. She was addictive. Her beauty was consuming. Her personality was enthralling. He couldn't stop thinking about her afterward. And, apparently, the feeling was mutual as she began calling his work number regularly, setting up future "service calls."

The only phone number Tom had for Julia was the disposable cell phone that she used for her secret lovers. She told Tom he should do the same so the two could keep the affair from his wife and explained to him her process of buying everything in cash. Over the months he had seen Julia quite a bit, telling Lisa he was on service calls or out of town on work related trips. He had become absolutely smitten by her and realized he had fallen in love.

Julia had always talked about how she was afraid of her husband. She had always told Tom he beat her and if he ever found out about their affair he would kill them both. Tom bought into this even though he had never observed any signs of physical injury on Julia, but then he had bought into everything else Julia told him as well. Like that she loved him and that she wished they could be together someday. In the past two months she had ramped up her stories of physical and mental abuse. She claimed Carlos would beat her and rape her each night. She said he was an alcoholic and he would drink so much he would be incapable of reasoning with. He would accuse her of infidelity and he would beat her for it. Tom was never a violent man, but the tales Julia spun enraged him. Such a beautiful, angelic woman; he could not understand the monster that would intentional inflict pain upon her.

When Ashley died, Tom's whole life and way of thinking changed. He was in a constant state of pain and sorrow. What was already a failing marriage became worse, at least in his eyes. He became emotionally numb. Nothing mattered to him anymore. That is, except for Julia. After the shock subsided, he finally contacted her and explained what had happened. He began seeing her again shortly after that, when he would tell Lisa he had gone to the office at night, not that she noticed. Julia told him tales of how the abuse had gotten worse. How she now very seriously feared for her life. She told Tom that in a drunken haze Carlos had tried to strangle her but she was able to kick him in the groin and get away.

Tom had had enough. Enough of the hurt and the pain inflicted on those he loved. He viewed the world differently now—there was a tremendous amount of evil in it that he had never known existed. He no longer gave society the benefit of the doubt. There were evil men out there that wanted nothing more than to take those he loved from him. Not this time, not ever again. The two hatched a plan to execute Carlos. The first order of business was to find a gun. Julia had determined the best place to purchase a gun would be a drug riddled neighborhood she knew of in Davie.

Julia recalled how Vikki had been mugged years ago when walking from the bar where she worked to her car after her shift. She had told Julia one of the bar backs at work had given her a gun to keep in her purse and that he had gotten it from a drug dealer in Davie. That bar back was now a bartender at the same bar, and Julia asked him one night where in Davie she could get good cocaine. She said she heard he knew a guy there years ago, to which he acknowledged he did and told her the neighborhood she needed to go to, but strongly advised against going there alone. She failed to share the bartender's warning with Tom before he ventured out, however.

As Tom pulled up on J Street, he was overcome by doubt and fear. He had never seen anything like the neighborhood he was in now, at least not in person. He knew he was already standing out. He thought about bailing, but quickly regained his nerve by remembering his purpose. He was there to save the life of someone he loved. Something he had failed to do once before, but would not fail at again.

A very large black man casually approached his car. Tom asked for Jemile, but quickly found out through a string of profanity that Jemile was not there and he would have to deal with the large gentleman before him named Dantrelle. He made his request known to Dantrelle, and while he waited for him to get the handgun, he looked at the different houses in the neighborhood. His eyes focused in on a rundown home just a few houses away. Yellow caution tape tied to the mailbox in the front corner of the property flapped in the wind. He assumed some type of gang crime had occurred there and didn't focus much more attention on it. He had no idea that this home had been the location of two recent homicides that had nothing to do with gang violence.

With the gun secured, the pair continued with their plan to eradicate the world of an evil man. They discussed several different possibilities and the inherent risks to all of them. One plan seemed the safest and that was the one Tom had carried out flawlessly thus far.

Julia, of course, needed an alibi and set up the appointment at the salon with Vikki. As soon as she left, she phoned Tom on the disposable cell phones, which because both had paid cash for them and the prepaid minutes, couldn't be traced to either of them. Tom had already been in the Coral Gables area, parked in a restaurant parking lot approximately one half mile from the entrance to Las Islas. He left his car there and walked to the house. Though the entrance had a security guard working at it at all times, there was also a footpath entrance that was just out of view of the guard, a flaw in the community's design that a vast majority of homeowners regularly complained about. Clean cut Tom, dressed in his khaki pants and blue polo shirt, a ball cap and backpack, seemed to blend in with the residents of the posh community. He walked to the Hernandez residence with little fanfare or recognition.

Once there he gave a quick glance around the surrounding yards and up and down the street. It appeared to be clear. He quickly swung the backpack off his shoulders and reached into one of the smaller front compartments for the surgical gloves. He then pulled out a small black handgun from a different compartment and put it down to his side, trying his best to conceal it if anyone happened to come by. With the other hand he dug into his pants pocket and pulled out a house key, given to him by Julia.

Once inside the foyer he had to determine where Julia's husband was. Julia had expected him to be home all afternoon, but if Tom had discovered him to be gone from the house, he was to call her and let her know, then lie in wait somewhere on the first floor. Julia had said that if he was home as expected, he would most likely be in his office, where he spent the majority of his time. It didn't take long for Tom to verify that she was correct. He heard Carlos call out to his wife, telling Tom his exact location. He sharpened his focus. This monster, Tom thought, would get what he deserved.

Tom approached slowly, his finger on the trigger. He tried to imitate police officers he had seen on television; it was the only frame of reference he had. He looked like Don Johnson minus the flashy suit as he slowly walked down the hall, arms bent, barrel of the gun pointed to the ceiling. Finally, he turned the corner and stood in the doorway of the office. He saw Carlos for the first time. Their eyes met. He remembered the look of surprise on his face. He pulled the trigger. Tom was amazed at how easy it was. He had never fired a gun before and he hadn't known what to expect. He didn't know if he would miss, or if there would be an alarming recoil after firing. The flash of the gun went off and in that quick moment before Tom knew his aim had been true, he thought of Ashley. If she had given a momentary look of surprise when she saw a monster before her, about to take her life. But Ashley had been an innocent victim; the man now bleeding on the floor was not. And Tom hadn't made the man suffer as Ashley had; it was all over in an instant.

They had decided that Tom should leave the gun behind to make it look like a professional hit. Tom had seen a lot of gangster shows and movies and that was always what professional hit men did. He would drop the gun where he stood and quickly leave. Julia had told Tom that a hit would be believable to police because she claimed Carlos gambled a lot. She also claimed he had had many affairs with married women.

Tom felt he should change afterword because he expected to be covered in blood. When he discovered he didn't have a drop on him, at least that he noticed, he debated momentarily if he should change or just leave the house quickly. Ultimately, he changed into the shorts and t-shirt because he felt he might appear as two different people to anyone who had seen him come in and leave. If police questioned neighbors they would get two different descriptions of someone walking alone.

Once back to his car, Tom called Julia and told her it was over. She was still at the salon and didn't say much other than, OK, thank you, and then she hung up. He felt no remorse as he drove home, just anger. Anger for a world that could create such monsters. In that brief instant in which their eyes met, he thought he remembered seeing fear in the eyes of his victim. He superimposed that look on the image he had of his daughter. He began to weep. His whole life was different now. He was a different Tom Wooten. There were no simple joys in life anymore.

Despite feeling confident he had left no evidence of himself behind, he still would have the worry every day for the rest of his life that he could be found out and go to jail. And what now for Lisa? He had done this act to save Julia's life, at least that's what he told himself. But he had also done it so they could be together. Julia's name had been left out of Jim Brekenridge's notebook. Tom knew she wasn't involved in Ashley's disappearance. Of all his previous mistresses, she was the only one he truly cared about. The only one he loved and saw a future with. He knew he couldn't be with Lisa anymore, even if she wanted to stay with him after finding out about his affairs, which he wasn't sure she knew about because she was still heavily medicated and they rarely spoke. He certainly hadn't told her of them.

He shook all these thoughts from his head for an instant and was hit with a moment of clarity, a sort of enlightenment. He was completely unrecognizable to who he had been just a month ago. He had thought that before but now he could see it in his mind, he could picture two images of himself. He could see himself smiling, sitting at the dining room table watching Ashley. He could see Lisa walking, talking, alert. Happy. He golfed, he worked in peace, he did fun things and took pleasure in them. And then he saw what he had become. What he was at that moment. Tears streaming down his cheeks. Paranoia setting in. There was nothing to look forward to and now no way to even attempt to salvage and rebuild the life he had once known. With what he had just done he had hitched his horse to one very distinctive wagon, Julia's. And it was all or nothing.

CHAPTER 19

Jim finally got the call he had been waiting for, not that he could be excited about it. He had already been told of Louis's suicide via a phone call from Jorge. The two men, at least at that time, were still at odds over what crime Louis was ultimately good for, but that would soon change. Two days after discovering Louis's decomposing body, Jorge had gotten word from the crime lab that the DNA retrieved from the back of Anne's neck had been analyzed and a profile had indeed been created as he had hoped. That profile was then compared to the DNA profile of Louis Bradford. They were not a match. Jorge was crushed. Anne's DNA had been located on the bottom of Louis's shoes, along with some dirt and a type of green algae, but he knew it meant nothing to his case. Louis had admitted to hovering over Anne's body when he found her.

But the bad news for Jorge didn't stop there. The hairs collected in the garage during the initial search did not match those of the South Florida Strangler's victims either. As devastating as it was to Jorge, being a man of true humility and integrity, he called Jim right away, as he said he would, to let him know that he had been wrong: Louis Bradford was not his guy. That Jim's theory seemed more likely.

Jim immediately requested the DNA collected from Louis Bradford's apartment and car be tested against Ashley's DNA profile. Not only did Ashley's DNA match what was found in Louis's apartment, but one of the hairs collected and analyzed matched hers as well. This, however, did not prove to be the only evidence. The fibers collected from Ashley's body matched a quilt found in Louis's car and the green algae found on the bottom of Louis's shoe also was consistent with algae found in the waters of the canal where her body had been found.

When that phone call finally came telling Jim this, that he had found the murderer of an innocent child, it was bittersweet. There would be no arrest. He wouldn't get to slap handcuffs on the person who had done this. In that way he felt justice couldn't ever be fully served. But Jim saw the bigger picture as well. He knew that Louis Bradford's fate would have been the same had the state of Florida been the one to impose it on him, and that even though Louis had had the power to choose it on his own, he had still gotten what he deserved.

The skeletons found in Louis's backyard, three in all, all were identified through DNA as missing children from Broward County. Julie Burrell was five when Louis lured her into his car at a local park, pleading with her to help find his dog. Karen Schierholtz was eight when Louis stopped her as she walked to school in the rain and asked if she wanted a ride. Michelle Cain was six when she asked Louis for help finding her parents at the beach. Despite only four of his victims ever being found, two others were linked to him through the DNA left behind. They had been missing children up to that point, but now those families could at least have closure. And the other two children Louis had abducted, brutalized, and murdered would forever remain missing as he had been quite successful in making them completely disappear.

After dismissing Louis as his prime suspect, Jorge wouldn't have to wait long for a new one. Less than a week after finding out the man he suspected of being the serial killer he had been chasing was actually a serial killer someone else was chasing, he and the rest of his group were called to the taskforce headquarters in Miami for a briefing. As the room filled and the two obligatory raspberry donuts remained, Lieutenant Greer took his position behind the podium. He explained about Carlos Hernandez's murder and a picture of Carlos appeared on a slide show he had put together. The picture was from his driver's license; he was smiling. He looked like a regular guy. Jorge remembered him and was surprised by his murder. It had gotten some attention in the Miami area because of Carlos's status as a doctor and his wealth, but not the same amount of attention in Broward County and so Jorge knew nothing of it until then. He became anxious as he waited to hear how it tied in to the Strangler killings.

The next photo was a crime scene photo of Carlos as he lay dead on the carpet of his office. Lieutenant Greer began to slowly, thoroughly explain the investigation into Carlos's death. He explained how his wife had found him and could think of no one who wanted to hurt such a gentle man. He explained about the gun being left at the scene and the early indication being that it was a professional hit. He told of a locked desk drawer in the room Carlos had been found and how, when opened, a cigar box full of pill bottles was discovered. And then he read the names on the pill bottles. Jorge began to perspire. His mouth went dry. Had he really shaken the hand of a killer, looked him square in the eyes, and not only not known it was him, but actually complimented him? He felt embarrassed yet again and sunk down in his seat.

Of course, as time passed Carlos was determined to be the South Florida Strangler. His DNA matched what was retrieved from Anne's body and when truly investigated, the links between Carlos and the victims became apparent. Most importantly the murder weapon was located where it had always been kept, under the driver's side front seat of his car. The fibers of the pantyhose had maintained DNA profiles from some of his victims and that was the smoking gun needed to name Carlos Hernandez publicly as the South Florida Strangler. The name of one of Florida's most notorious serial killers was finally known. Posthumously, Carlos finally got the recognition he craved for himself and not his alter ego.

The only murder never connected to Carlos was Rebecca Sullivan. Mika Jackson remained incarcerated for it until his death at age thirty-eight when he was bludgeoned by another inmate. The South Florida Strangler had finally claimed his last victim.

After Carlos was officially known as the South Florida Strangler, the taskforce disbanded. There was only one murder left to solve, and despite it being handled by taskforce members and not the detectives who were initially assigned it, it was not investigated with the same gusto as their victim's victims had been. The media sensationalized Carlos's death at first, but as time went on the murder of Carlos Hernandez became less important than the acts he committed while alive. The investigation itself was headed by Detective Tony Petrulia.

Tony had bought in immediately to the idea that someone had discovered Carlos was the South Florida Strangler, a loved one of a victim perhaps, and taken revenge against him. He cared very little about the case and harbored resentment towards it and its victim. His enjoyable run in the taskforce was over and he would soon have to go back to reality, both at home and at work. It was his opinion the killing was done by a professional, hence no sign of forced entry, the use of an unregistered weapon, and the lack of physical evidence left behind.

Julia had been considered a suspect initially, but she was quickly crossed off the list. Her alibi had checked out and, most importantly, Tony was more interested in trying to sleep with her than connecting her to the crime.

And knowing she had another one on the hook, Julia played the game with him. She would have slept with him if it came to that and she found it necessary, but thankfully for her it never did.

Two months into the investigation Tony was involved in a car accident while at work. He was drug tested as a result and was subsequently suspended for testing positive for steroids, as well as ecstasy and cocaine. An internal affairs investigation of Tony ensued and, after several months, it was discovered he had also leveraged his position of authority into sexual relations with numerous women, dating back to his second year of duty. Tony was subsequently arrested on abuse of power charges and several counts of rape. He ended up taking a plea bargain and served twelve years in prison.

The detective who picked up Carlos's murder investigation discovered Tony had literally taken no notes. Interviews, specifically with Julia, were not recorded in any way. Try as he might, he knew making a case against anyone would be difficult, and the case ultimately went unsolved.

Jorge went back to his capacity as a Pembroke Pines detective and was promoted to sergeant three years later.

Despite his successes over the remainder of his career, Jorge was always haunted by the idea that he had been so wrong about Louis Bradford. Maybe if he hadn't been, Jim would have been able to build a case against him before he had a chance to take his own life. Maybe if he had seen something, some type of sign when he met Carlos Hernandez, it all could have been avoided. Both men would be in jail and not dead. It knocked down his confidence as a police officer and he would never regain it as long as he worked.

Jim's case load began piling up again. The Wooten case was the last kidnapping and child murder he ever worked, and he was glad about it. Lost in the rollercoaster that was the Ashley Wooten case was the actual rescue of another little girl. Both Jim and Dan received commendations for their involvement in the Heather Martin rescue. Jim was voted police officer of the year for the county for his coordination of the rescue. He was finally able to take pride in it. To feel good that he had helped someone. Both the Ashley Wooten and Heather Martin cases made Jim a better father, at least that's what he would always tell people. He enjoyed time with his girls a lot more after that. Jim continued solving cases, pissing people off, and alienating himself from his co-workers until he retired at age fifty-five, still a detective.

Dan remained a detective for two years after the Wooten case then was promoted to sergeant. He and Jim remained friendly, and as fate would have it, toward the end of Jim's career, Dan was transferred back to the detective bureau and took the position once held by Sergeant Phillips; he had become Jim's boss. At first Dan was excited about it. He felt a sense of satisfaction that he would finally have the say he never had working as Jim's partner. He was finally going to be the one running the show. Sadly, he realized he was wrong very quickly.

As for Jemile, the Broward County Sheriff's Office made good on their word to help him with his charges for the assistance he gave in closing not one, but two serial killer cases. Jemile served only six months and returned back to the house on J Street.

During his six month incarceration, Jemile's operation was overtaken by one of the local gangs and they weren't too pleased at Jemile's insistence that he be included in their now larger operation. A month after his release, Jemile was shot and killed in a drive by shooting. No arrest was ever made for his murder.

It didn't take long for Julia to drop Tom. She had no use for him now; he had served his purpose. She was cold and she was hurtful when she told him of this decision. She told him if he didn't accept that they wouldn't be together she would turn him in to the police. And that was that; they never spoke again.

Julia never came under the suspicion she should have in Carlos's death. Partly because of the damage to the investigation done by Tony, but also because of her genuine reaction to the news that Carlos was a serial killer. That particular interview came early on, in the presence of multiple task force members, including Lieutenant Greer. There was no acting necessary when it came to that interrogation. She was speechless initially. Then she simply denied that it was true. She pondered how it could have happened without her knowledge. But it didn't take long for the pieces to fit. She had always believed Carlos was cheating on her when he was out at night under the guise of work, but now she knew what he was really doing.

She was hurt when the shock wore off. Her narcissistic nature allowed her to question how he could do that to her. How he could kill people and keep such secrets from her. It never entered her mind that she had no right to be hurt by his secrets or his actions. That not only had she kept secrets of her own, but she had been responsible for taking a life as well: his.

Satisfied she had no part in the South Florida Strangler killings, or the murder of her husband, she was never questioned about either again.

Julia's beauty added to the sensationalism that surrounded Carlos's death and discovery as the Strangler. National news outlets found her intriguing. She wasn't what they had expected from a serial killer's wife. She wasn't mousy or abused or fearful. She was vibrant and gorgeous and alive. She began making media appearances and loving every minute of it. She no longer had to play the grieving widow. She could be someone who was angry, who despised her husband for who he was.

The money Carlos had sought to get her in his passing with the massive life insurance policy actually provided her with very little. Lawsuits on behalf of his victim's families ate up the majority of it. However, she kept the house, and she made more than she ever needed by doing talk show interviews, reality television, even writing a book. She now had everything she ever wanted. Fame. Money. Freedom. No one ever suspected the truth: that she was the femme fatale behind the death of a serial killer.

Tom, too, had dealt with the shock of discovering that the man he had murdered was a serial killer. In reality it helped him to breathe a little easier. Thinking of all the murders Carlos had been responsible for and all the people who hated him because of them, he felt it would be harder now for police to discover he was involved. They would have a massive suspect pool by his estimation. He also felt less guilty knowing the life he had taken belonged to a truly evil man. A man much like the one who had murdered his daughter.

Depression swept over him after Julia broke things off. He questioned his whole life and if it was worth living. He became consumed by the past, reliving happier moments. He dwelled on that one day, that one instant in which his whole life changed. He dreamed of the ability to go back and change it. If he had just stayed home and not golfed. If he had been able to keep his phone turned on. It drove him near insanity. He still spoke with Mark and saw him occasionally, but their relationship was never the same. Mark had finally become what Tom once was: stable, reliable, the one to look up to. He had surpassed Tom and no longer needed to idolize him.

Tom would always feel both guilty and victimized. He realized that at times the supposed line between guilt and innocence, between victim and perpetrator became blurred.

At times he wondered if people had to be one or the other. He realized sometimes they were probably both. His life had become about one moment. Before that moment occurred he had been happy, he had been successful, he had hopes and ambitions, he was viewed as a good guy. After that moment occurred, his only hope was that he could somehow get back what he had before it.

Lisa Wooten eventually began putting her life back together. She had developed a strong dependency on sleeping pills and pain medications after Ashley's death, and after a few months her sister began trying to wean her off them, which took some time and persistence. This, of course, was when she found out about the extent of Tom's extra-marital affairs. She not only had to finally deal with the death of her daughter, but the dissolution of her marriage at the same time. But in time she was able to function again and she returned to her job, which had been waiting for her. One of the hardest things for her to accept was that she had actually met the man who kidnapped and murdered her daughter, and that she found him to be so normal. That she hadn't felt frightened by him at all. She realized in time that he was like a chameleon and had gained the trust of not only herself, but nearly everyone he had interacted with. She had solace in knowing he would never fool anyone again. That he would never hurt anyone again.

She moved in with her sister until she could get back on her feet emotionally and financially, and she and Tom divorced four months after Ashley's death. The divorce was amicable and relatively uncontested, without a custody battle, although Lisa refused to speak to Tom and rarely looked in his direction. They did unite for one final act as a family about two weeks after their divorce: to clean out Ashley's room. Neither had had the heart or stomach to do it before this, but since their divorce and Tom's decision to sell the house, they knew they needed to do it now and it was something Lisa felt she should be a part of. It was torturous. It was gut wrenching. It was final. She was officially gone now, Lisa thought. Her things were packed in boxes and given to a local Goodwill store, except for a few items Lisa and Tom had taken for themselves. Eventually Lisa was able to rent her own place, and on her bedroom dresser, mixed in with various framed pictures, sat a few stuffed animals and one white patent leather shoe.

John Scanlan is a police officer on the picturesque island of Palm Beach in South Eastern Florida. After moving south from the small, Western New York village of Le Roy in 2005, he subsequently fell in love with South Florida's tropical beauty and laidback lifestyle, which is the backdrop for his first novel, *Of Guilt and Innocence*. A graduate of Brockport College, John's previous endeavors include training with the United States Border Patrol in Charleston, South Carolina and working as a legal aid for the former Immigration and Naturalization Service in Buffalo, New York. He currently resides in Palm Beach County, Florida with his wife and two small daughters.

Made in the USA
Charleston, SC
21 March 2014